A Kiss Worth Waiting For
Dan Valenti

Collar City Publishing—East Greenbush, NY
ISBN: 978-1-7370674-0-5
Library of Congress Control Number: 2021908041
Title: *A Kiss Worth Waiting For...*
Author: Dan Valenti
Digital distribution | 2021
Paperback | 2021

This is a work of fiction. The characters, names, incidents, places, and dialogue are products of the author's imagination, and are not to be construed as real.

"We all have a story. A tale of where we've come from and who we've been, that leads to where we are and who we are today."

Chapter 1

Descending upon the Verona Airport is always a magnificent sight. The harbor is peaceful and beautiful. So many colorful fishing boats, the lakeside promenade lined with restaurants, even in the summer this town remains relatively calm and makes for an idyllic place to relax.

Bardolino has been my home for the last five years, and this will be the second summer my granddaughter is spending it with me.

Even though it has been a long flight from Avon, Connecticut where Angelina lives with my son and his wife, she summons up a burst of energy and is glued to the window taking in the breathtaking site.

Last year she was only supposed to stay for two weeks, but she fell in love with Italy just as I did, so we extended her visit to a month. During that time, she made several friends, and since they spoke English as their second language, they began teaching her how to speak Italian. This was all the more reason Angelina pleaded with her parents to let her come spend most of her summer vacation with me again.

The landing was not very smooth, and Angelina looked at me with concern. I put my arm around her and smiled assuring her we were fine. It comforted her immediately. We both could not wait to stand up, stretch, and depart the plane.

As we walked towards baggage claim, Angelina was soaking it all in. Her little pink backpack bouncing up and down because of her energetic pace. Her happiness brings me so much joy.

Angelina was now 12 years old, but with a much more mature intellect. She loves to learn, ask questions, analyze, and figure things out. She also loves to be told stories, especially from me.

Ever since she was about 2 years old, I began telling her stories. Not so much from story books, except for the occasional holiday ones where I loved telling her about Santa Claus and his elves, but from my own life experiences. There is a special box I have which contains very personal things to me, including one postcard from every place I have ever visited. I have acquired quite a collection over the past thirty years since my job had me travelling 80% of the time. I would let her pick out a postcard, and then I would tell the story behind it.

As we made our way out of the airport, I hailed a taxi, and we began our short 9-mile trip home.

I prefer flying into Milan airport, which is around a 60-mile drive to my home. Although longer, it is a much more beautiful ride. But I knew Angelina would not want to be cooped up in a car for another hour after a long flight, so I chose Verona airport instead.

After some small talk with the driver, my property came into view. We pulled up to the gates and I punched in the code, the large gates opened, and we proceeded down the mile-long driveway.

I am still taken back by this enormous 3000-acre vineyard I now call home after fifty-five years of living in the states. It was a dream come true when I purchased it five years ago. I knew nothing about growing grapes, or the process of making the wine, only that I was a wine lover and had this new ambition since my official retirement.

Five years ago, I rented a villa in a local town, Torri de Benaco, for a month. It was shortly after I had retired and a long-awaited vacation I had planned. That was when I stumbled upon what some people would call a deal of a lifetime. The vineyard was just up for sale. The man who built and ran it for 55 years, had two children, and neither wanted the family business. He did not want the vineyard to be leveled and villas scattered amongst the property as one real estate developer wanted to do, nor did he want to sell to one of the large commercial wineries. So, one evening, he and I were the only two sitting at a local osteria and we began talking. His name was Vito and he spoke very broken English and my Italian was not so good. But, with the help of the bartender we had an amazing conversation. He was genuine, sincere, and passionate about his life's work. He was willing to make a deal with the right person. I showed a great deal of interest and let him know the towns my grandparents left years ago to make a new life in the United States. That bit of information established an instant connection between us. He agreed to meet me the next day and give me a tour of his vineyard. I stayed awake almost until dawn going over my finances, trying to figure out if I wanted to invest such a large amount of

2

money into a business, I knew virtually nothing about. The next day I met him at the vineyard. Vito gave me an incredibly detailed and well-informed tour while we talked for hours. His son, Fernando, was there and he spoke English very well, which helped the flow of the conversation. My career taught me how to process large amounts of information and mentally file it so I may come back to each file individually as needed, and it sure came in handy since this information was all new to me and somewhat overwhelming considering the substantial financial obligation that would be attached to my final decision.

The land had an amazing productive and profitable vineyard, a large main house, and a smaller guest house where a family of eight lived. That family worked the entire wine making process from vines and grapes to bottling, labeling, and packing. Vito made it clear, the family stays employed with the same arrangements he had made with them years ago. I assured him I would keep the family, same deal he had with them, keep everything the same, and not dishonor his 55 years of hard work. Vito was a hardened self-made man of values and integrity. He looked into my eyes and could tell I was sincere. We worked out a deal and shook hands. I spent the next day examining the books along with a local accountant I hired, before deciding to sign any documents. A few days later we settled things with an attorney and bank.

Now, this beautiful place was mine, and a wonderful escape for my family and grandchildren to make memories.

As the car stopped in front of the house Angelina jumped out and started running towards her friend Lucia. As they collided into a hug they just about toppled over. Lucia, 13, is the youngest daughter of Franco and Maria Martone, the family that runs the vineyard.

The driver unloaded the luggage from the trunk, I paid him, and he slowly drives off, as a small cloud of dust followed him back down the long driveway.

I wave to the girls as they head towards the swings. Franco saw the car and was making his way up to the house to greet me. He helped me carry the suitcases inside and filled me in on whatever I may have missed over the past two weeks I had been in the states. He then invited Angelina and I to dinner, in which I graciously accepted.

3

Chapter 2

Dinner was amazing. Franco's wife Maria, and oldest daughter Isabella prepared homemade meals that compared to the best restaurants I have ever been to. Franco and Maria had broken English, but their children all spoke it very well. They were all extremely hard dedicated workers. I did not like to consider them employees, because they have become more like family to me.

I was not a very trusting person. It took a lot to gain my trust, and this family has.

After good conversation and an amazing dessert, Angelina and I jumped into my favorite UTV, the Ranger Crew XP1000, and headed up to our home. This vehicle is a must for getting around the terrain of the vineyard and trails around the outskirts.

After cleaning up and getting ready for bed, we met down in the sitting room. It is a great place to relax and just enjoy the calmness. The large stone fireplace almost covers one wall and keeps the entire downstairs warm during the winter months. The furniture is all oversized and extremely comfortable. Several lamps provided just enough light, and there is a beautiful wood trunk filled with warm blankets.

Even though we were both tired from an awfully long day, Angelina asked if I would tell her a story. "Of course," I replied. "You know where the box is."

She went to the small table near the bookshelf and opened it up, she took out a handful of postcards, shuffled through them before finding one that sparked her interest. She put the rest back, closed the box, got herself a blanket and came over to the sofa and nestled in next to me. "Here you are grandpa," handing me the postcard. I looked at it, and my mind flashed back to the time I got that card.

Now you must understand that most of the postcards in that box did not have good memories for me. They were to remind me of places and events that chartered my life and made me the person I am today.

My career with the CIA took me to many of these places, so I would need to candy-coat the story as much as possible.

I held the postcard. "Venezuela." "Well, on this trip we had to leave in the middle of the night. We flew out of Delaware in a large cargo aircraft called an L 100-30 and made our way out to the Caribbean Sea. Two and a half hours later we were descending towards Caracas, the capital of Venezuela. Our mission was to rescue several US diplomats, including two of our own guys. The US was preparing for a possible military intervention and we needed to get these Americans out fast.

Our plane had a commercial registration number on its side, so airport officials had no idea what was going on, they just assumed we were a commercial plane. We landed, lowered the ramp, and drove our vehicle right off the plane and headed towards the US Embassy. The four-person crew stayed on board and secured the plane. The six diplomats were waiting and in fear of their lives at the embassy. Caracas was one of the most dangerous capital cities in the world. We made our way through the dark streets, occasionally we would hear a gunshot, not aimed at us, but in the near distance. Luckily, we had a large eight passenger bullet proof hummer, made and designed specifically for these sorts of missions. We were being guided by GPS, but my partner and I had studied all possible ways in and out of the area just in case we needed to change course in a moment's notice. The embassy was now in site, and we called to make sure they were ready to go. They had already erased all data from the computers and secured all areas just in case the embassy was invaded. As we were pulling up to the rear of the building, we noticed four men standing outside a car, they were all armed with assault rifles. This was not uncommon to see in Caracas, but these men were here for a reason, to make sure nobody left or entered the embassy. They were the bad guys.

We turned off the head lights and crept slowly towards the door where we were picking up the assets. The four men were laughing and talking loudly, unaware of what was going on. The door opened, and I jumped out to usher the five men and one woman into our vehicle. The heavy steel building door made a slamming noise as it closed, and the four men nearby heard it, suddenly their laughter turned to silence as they saw our vehicle. They started shouting in Spanish, stop or we will shoot, then began shooting. We knew we had to stop this now or it would lead into a high-speed chase through the city and we did not want that attention.

So, I took out my gun, lowered my bullet proof window and shot at the tires of their car blowing out two of them. That ended any chase that would have pursued.

My partner quickly maneuvered through the streets and GPS had us at 11 minutes estimated time arrival back to our plane. I noticed a small corner store and told my partner to pull over, reluctantly he did so. I ran inside and got this postcard. "

Angelina's eyes widened and she smiled.

"Then I got back into the vehicle and called the pilot, he never turned off the engines because he knew this mission would be under 30 minutes if all went well.

Suspicions were now being raised at the airport and the pilot said a security vehicle was heading out to investigate the plane. We were now two minutes away. Speeding would only raise more suspicion, so we were driving a conservative speed. We were now coming up on the security car which had flashing blue lights on the roof. Again, I took my gun out and fired two bullets blowing out both rear tires of the security car, it spun out of control and went off into the grassy field. My partner drove up the ramp and into the plane. The pilot immediately began raising the ramp as he turned the massive plane and asked for clearance to depart.

There was silence on the other end, and he requested clearance for departure again. A voice responded asking the pilot to identify himself. The pilot responded with a playbook response, meaning it was not the truth but answered the question.

At this point we were lining up to take off with or without permission. I told the pilot to get us out of here. He was stopped, configured the flaps, and started accelerating, he was at 140mph when he was finally cleared to depart, and at 160mph we lifted off. At that point everyone started to breathe again."

I pulled Angelina in a little tighter as we both laughed.

"And in a few hours, we were back in Delaware. Everybody safe and sound"

"Wow grandpa that sounded so intense."

"It sure was. Now what do you say we hit the sack? We had a long day and after breakfast in the morning we can take a ride around and make sure everything is operating as it should be."

"Can Lucia come with us?"

"Of course."

We got up and I walked Angelina to her bedroom, gave her a kiss on her forehead and whispered, "goodnight my little Angel."

"Goodnight grandpa."

I sat at my desk and shuffled through some papers before retiring for the night.

Chapter 3

I was up early the next day. Somehow, years ago, I became accustomed to sleeping no more than five hours. Some nights are very restful, and some are tormented by nightmares of my past.

Soon I heard Angelina's footsteps racing down the stairs. We had a small breakfast, her favorite cereal, and a few scrambled eggs and toast for me.

The round eight-person kitchen table was situated in front of the large double window, with an amazing view of the town below. The grassy hill covered with stones of all shapes and sizes went on for miles before reaching any civilization.

Angelina was the only family to visit me here in four years. Both of my children have their own young families, homes, and careers in the states. My son Vincent and his wife Marla settled in Connecticut where they met in college. They are both architects and formed a partnership business. Marla is an interior designer, and Vincent is a residential architect.

My daughter Emery and her husband Mark began dating in high school, then went to local colleges in New York where we lived.

Emery became a clothing designer, while Mark became an environmental engineer. They moved to Ft. Collins CO shortly after graduation and both found great jobs in their respective fields. They used money from their wedding to put a down payment on a nice home in a picturesque residential area, and have a beautiful eight-year-old girl, Giovanna.

Just as we were cleaning up the table, we heard a faint knock on the front door, Angelina ran to the door, knowing it would be Lucia.

"Grandpa, we will be on the front porch!"

"OK, I'm coming."

I walked out and closed the door. "Buongiorno signore," said Lucia.

"Buongiorno." I responded

"Come on girls lets go for a ride."

My UTV has six bucket seats, so of course the girls took the two in the far back. We proceeded to drive all around the vineyard. I knew enough about the growing process by now to see that everything was looking healthy and it seems like we would have a good season ahead.

Throughout the ride we came across Salvatore and Angelo, two of Lucia's older brothers who along with Franco, oversee the entire operation.

I stop and have a conversation with each of them. They are deeply passionate about their work. For this Martone family it is a generational compelling saga. Franco is fourth generation, and his children fifth generation winemakers.

Winemaking is a science. The selection of the fruit, the precise time to harvest, crushing and pressing, fermentation, clarification, aging and bottling, this family knows every step and has mastered it. I knew practically nothing about the winemaking process when I bought this place. The Martone's have taught me so much, yet there is so much more for me to learn from them.

I soon dropped Lucia off at her home. I promised Angelina I would take her into town to do some shopping and have lunch.

I normally do not like small vehicles but in Italy I find it is much easier to maneuver along some of the narrower roads with one. Angelina just loves the convertible custom shark gray colored Porsche, probably because the wind blows her hair all around and reminds her of a ride at an amusement park, I am sure.

Bardolino is a small village with quite a few shops selling everything from clothing to food. We strolled in and out of a few shops so she can pick out a few cute little things for her parents, and even something for her little cousin Giovanna.

We settle on a little café with a beautiful view of Lake Garda. Most of the people in town know who I am, but I am an introvert, and still adjusting to their way of life, so I keep things to a minimum, and that is respected.

My wine is sold in all the restaurants and cafes here and throughout most of Italy.

Angelina orders a small bowl of pasta noodles with salad; I settle for a chicken and pasta dish.

"Grandpa, don't you get lonely living here with no family?"

"Sometimes I do. I miss you, and your parents and your aunt Emery and Giovanna."

"Do you ever miss Grandma?"

"I do, but we just weren't a right fit, and she's happier now I'm sure."

Angelina just nodded as she sipped her lemonade and chewed on a little slice of bread.

My ex-wife and I decided on a mutual divorce when Emery was just 15 yrs. old, and Vincent was 17.

My career kept me traveling so much and hardened me emotionally in many ways I was told. She did not want a life with an absent husband and father, gone for months at a time. We slowly morphed into a compromising relationship and in the end, it is what brought upon the divorce. The perks of comfort just could not compare to having a genuine connection.

Since being in Italy I have had a few dates, but nothing really beyond that. I travel to the states a few times a year, but never long enough to develop a relationship, perhaps a dinner date here or there.

Being in the Intelligence community can be a very lonely career. Most do not make it past 10 yrs. Not everyone is cut out to be an agent. Usually, it's you and you alone. No back up, no team, and no brother in arms to help or bolster your effort. Some experiences take you to a place where mentally you can never be the same again. You become less human but learn to disguise who you have become.

An experienced career spy lives by a color code system. There are four levels, and we are always in one of these conditions. White, yellow, orange, red, with red being the lethal mode. As a result of an evolutionary process, enter the fifth condition, black. It is a place in combat where you cease to exist. By you, the conscious you, the thinking you, the you that you know. All cognitive operations cease to register. There is no thinking, no decision making, no internal dialogue, no reasoning, no regard for safety and most importantly, NO FEAR. There is only NOW, state of pure survival. It is an experience that is pure and powerful, shocking, yet exhilarating, and in the end.... alluring and addicting. To be in such a state of existence, where there is only pureness of action, where no thoughts can occur is an experience that is rarely visited by some and never experienced by most.

Chapter 4

After lunch we walked around a little more before driving back home. Lucia saw us coming up the driveway and made her way over to the house. Angelina asked if they could play outside for a little while.

"Of course," I responded.

I walked inside and into my office. I could see the answering machine blinking on my private line. One message was from my daughter in law, and one from an old friend, who works in the State Department. I knew he would be arriving in Italy soon to visit the embassy in Rome. He would like to visit me to discuss a few things. You may retire, but you never quite leave the intel community.

I was able to get some work done as Angelina and Lucia spent time outside. Soon it was dinner time for Lucia and Angelina came inside.

"Angelina," I called out.

"Yes grandpa?"

"Your mom left a message for you to call her."

Angelina came into the office and I dialed the number. The time difference is 6 hrs. so it is 10:15pm in CT.

It has only been a few days, but they miss her so much. Angelina clicked it over to speakerphone so I could join the conversation and answer the normal questions from my son and Marla.

"Yes, the flights were smooth, no delays, and Angelina is a complete joy, thank you again for letting her spend this time with me here."

After the call, I made us a light meal since she was not that hungry. I could hear her laughing with one of her girlfriends back home as they skyped. Soon the call ended, and I was waiting for her at the table. We talked and ate as she told me about how funny her friend was from back home.

After dinner and loading the dishwasher, we both went and sat on the sofa and turned on the TV to see if we could find anything Angelina would enjoy. There did not seem to be anything good on.

"How about a story?" She smiled and turned off the TV.

"OK, go pick a card."

She went to the box and returned with a postcard. I took it and looked. The beautiful Saint Basil's Cathedral.

She sat down next to me, and I wrapped my left arm around her. I took a sip of wine from my glass, closed my eyes, and began to tell her just one story from the several I have had in Russia.

"This photo is of Saint Basil's Cathedral in Russia. It is now a museum, situated right near the Kremlin, in Moscow

"What's the Kremlin?"

"It's like our White House, it's where the Russian president lives."

"So, my agency had been tracking a Russian agent for a few years. She frequently visited the US as a diplomat."

"There are women agents also grandpa?"

"Oh yes."

"She was operating under the cover of diplomacy, which means she was representing Russia during visits to the United Nations. We discovered her cover because she was trying to influence American policy, and extremely interested in our policies towards Iran and Israel. So, I was placed into a similar diplomatic role and my job was to find out everything I could. This took me from New York to Russia several times. We got to know each other and even had a few dinners in Russia. I'm not a big fan of Russian food but they have a dish called pelmeni which is rather good."

"Pelmeni? That sounds Italian grandpa."

"Well, it is sort of Italian." I said laughing.

"It's like a pastry dumpling filled with a minced meat and served in a soup broth."

"I sensed Nadia suspected I may be an intelligence officer as well, so I had to be very cautious."

I had to be just as cautious telling my granddaughter this story. The Russian government is known to use beautiful women, like Nadia, as intelligence officers so they can use sexual activity or seduction to conduct espionage, which we refer to as sexpionage.

Many times, this technique works, but I have been in this game too long to fall for it. Instead, I set a trap for her.

"I had to be sure Nadia was indeed an agent. So, the morning before I was meeting her for dinner, I arranged to get her legend."

"What's a legend?"

"It's what Nadia claims to be her biography or background. Like where she has lived, worked, went to school, things like that. This way I had time to review it, and possibly catch her in a lie later."

"So that morning I was to meet another agent inside a coffee shop in a busy part of Moscow. He would be sitting at a table having coffee. If his newspaper was folded and placed on his left side, I knew it was OK to sit with him and he wasn't followed."

"That's so cool grandpa."

I smiled.

"So luckily it was properly positioned, and I sat with him for a quick cup of coffee and I left with the newspaper which had my information inside. This brief meeting is what we call a brush pass. And that evening at dinner I was able to catch Nadia in several lies. My goal now was to give her false information in the hopes she would suffer a major blowback which would land her in prison because the Russian government doesn't mess around."

"But why would you want her to go to prison grandpa?"

"Well, she has been spying on the US for a few years now, trying to discover military and political secrets to use against us, so I was going to give her a taste of her own medicine. So, I gave her some bad information that the US was planning to drop bombs at the materials receiving area in a huge mountain range controlled by the Russian military called the Yamantau mountains, where it is said Russia has an underground nuclear lab. But the US would be using planes disguised as Iran aircraft. Iran and Russia are allies."

"And did she go back and tell them that? What happened to her?"

"Yes, she went back and told them. It never happened and I heard she was thrown in jail. But even if she were not put in jail, she could never come back to the US because she would be arrested and tried for espionage, and her government would no longer trust her or find her credible. So, we won."

What I could not tell Angelina was that I set up Nadia to bring me to the real reason I was in Russia, to have her lead me to the person she answers to. He was one of the top officials of the G.R.U,

13

Russian military intelligence. Yes, she was in the Russian military. Russia will claim the G.R.U no longer exists but it does, and the director reports directly to the Minister of Defense, not the president of Russia.

The man she led me to was responsible for a lethal covert operation in the Ukraine which took the lives of several CIA and DIA officers, and he was the mastermind behind many other attacks against us and our allies. He was the second in command of the G.R.U. This was retaliation and removal of a major threat.

I needed to confirm my suspicion she was in the military intelligence. The housing in the Yamantau mountain range was in the north and south. She was familiar with it and at one point corrected me when I purposely made a false statement about the location of the operations area.

That night after dinner she made her move to meet him and share the information, I had given her. I shadowed her using a Russian asset posing as a cab driver. Finally, after almost 3 hours of trailing and waiting, the meeting was happening. A mission like this is built up for months sometimes years and when it boils down to it you have seconds to execute the plan. I had to act quickly and terminate three people and make it appear to be a robbery. The driver was first, then the high ranking official and Nadia was last. My ride was still waiting around the corner, having not heard anything due to my firearms silencer. The streets were somewhat busy and blanketed under the night sky. We quickly maneuvered through traffic, back into Moscow and to the US Embassy where I was staying. I quickly boarded a plane and, on my way back home. Mission accomplished.

"Grandpa that sounds so scary."

"Ha ha, it can be scary sometimes my little angel. It's been a long day; are you almost ready for bed?"

She took a few cookies from the kitchen and a big glass of water as I walked her to her room. Gave her a kiss on her forehead and whispered goodnight.

I poured myself another glass of wine and just sat in my favorite reclining chair staring at photos on this one wall, it was covered with photos of my children and grandchildren. I reminisce about how lucky I am to have such a precious family. Then I grieve the darkness and loneliness I live with inside each day. I miss the

14

company of a woman, the touch of a woman, the scent of a woman's perfume as I hold her close.

I finish my drink, walk to the kitchen and place the glass on the sink. I walk over to the box and place the postcard back inside. I close the lid and rest my hand on top. The story of my life is contained in this box. I close my eyes and take a deep breath, then turn and walk down to my room.

Chapter 5

A ngelina is an early riser like me, so we were both awake as the sun was rising over the eastern hills and peeking through the windows.

In Italy everything is much more relaxed and simpler compared to the US and how I lived my entire life up until these last five years.

I can already see Franco, Salvatore, and Angelo working. They start the day early, then take a long lunch consisting of a meal and nap, then return to finish out the day, and always have a family dinner. I love that about this country, family is so important, simple things matter most.

I had an afternoon meeting set up with my European distributer, so I asked Maria if she would not mind keeping an eye on Angelina, which of course was not a problem since she would be hanging out with Lucia anyway.

The skills I have learned and perfected over the years through rigorous training, academics, and life experiences have helped me greatly dealing with people and in the business world. I have learned to read body language, expressions, gestures, etc. and it has helped me immensely.

The European distributor prior to my recent one had been in the business an exceedingly long time and charged a higher percent than I was willing to continually pay. I spent time researching new upcoming distributors and interviewed several until finally finding a brother and sister taking over their father's business, and they were hungry to expand, aggressive and using their fathers good name and reputation to their advantage.

After a wonderful meeting, I decided I was going to increase production, and move my wines into newly expanding markets. Franco's sons, Salvatore and Angelo were eager to use several acres of land currently not being utilized to full capacity, this new move would now allow them to run with their ambition.

After the meeting I made a few calls and took care of some paperwork, then got into the UTV and drove down to get Angelina.

I thanked Maria for watching her then she invited us to dinner that evening. I graciously accepted. It would also be a good time to share the news with Salvatore and Angelo.

"Grandpa can Lucia and I swim for a little while?"

"Sure, if it's OK with you Maria."

"Si." She responded.

"Va bene!" I replied. Simply meaning OK!

The two girls got into the vehicle and we headed back up to the house. The girls changed in Angelina's room and headed out the back door leading to the deck and pool.

"Be careful, I'm going to get some drinks and meet you out there."

By nature, I am very over-protective of my children and grandchildren, always have been. My children still joke with me about it.

I changed into shorts, made a pitcher of lemonade and grabbed a few plastic cups and headed out. I would relax in the jacuzzi which overlooked the pool.

After the girls tired of swimming, they sat on the lounge chairs and enjoyed a glass of lemonade as the warm sun dried them off.

I made a comment to Angelina about going inside soon to get dressed for dinner. Lucia walked down the hill back to her home, we got ready and relaxed some more before driving down for dinner. I brought along a few bottles of wine.

Chapter 6

Maria, with the help from Isabella, always made the most amazing meals. Traditional family recipes could make even the simplest of meals taste amazing.

After dinner I mentioned the increase in production to Franco, and his thoughts of using the several acres of unharvested vines.

Franco and now his sons knew this land better than anyone, and what it could produce. We opened the discussion up to Salvatore and Angelo, who were very enthusiastic. It was decided we would harvest more and increase production.

The distributer told me the Bardolino sweet red wines were becoming more popular, especially amongst the younger people. We have never had problems selling our entire stock each year so this would be even more financially beneficial.

After a cup of coffee and a large slice of an amazing amaretto flavored cake that Isabella made, I said thank you to the family and went outside to let Angelina know we were heading home. She was playing some sort of game on the porch with Lucia and Antonella, Lucia's 15 yr. old sister.

"Good night girls."

"Good night signore!"

The girls seem to love speaking English, because except for me and Angelina, they probably do not use the language much.

Instead of going straight to the house we took a little ride around the property. I had updated many things since buying the vineyard to help production, bottling, labeling, and packaging run much smoother and more efficient.

When we made it back to the house Angelina took a shower and got ready for bed, as I checked emails. She then made her way to the living room where I was sitting with my laptop and she brought hers as well.

As much as I was against social media sites, I understood it was a way of communication between her and her friends.

I had an email from an old friend, Jim, who was now retired as well. He has been trying to come to Italy and visit for a few years, but it has not worked out for him because his wife had gone through a few serious health issues. But things are now better, and they want to take a vacation to Italy.

When working in the intelligence community you very seldom form close friendships. Things are very compartmentalized, and most are not fully aware of the entire picture. You have a specific job and that is what is expected of you. Everything else is on a need-to-know basis, and most never need to know. The players change quite often so you never form real friendships. I have only a few I would call true friends, but many I would consider close acquaintances spread out over many government agencies and private businesses both in the states and abroad, that I could trust and count on in a whim.

Jim and I worked together for years. Jim was what we called a "cobbler." His job was to create passports, visa's, driver's licenses, diplomas, and other such documents. He could create a whole new life and identity very quickly.

In especially hostile countries we would acquire an asset who would be willing to give up whatever bits of classified information they had just for a chance to get them and their families out of that country and to start over in a more non-tyrannical, democratically controlled country such as in the US.

If that classified information were deemed credible and helpful to our government, sometimes permission would be granted to help an asset escape his/her country by providing them the necessary credentials needed to get them started on a new life. That is when Jim's expertise was put to use. Time was of the essence in most situations like this. If the asset were exposed before they escaped, they would be tortured and most likely killed.

Some years ago, when I was asked to oversee what we call the Red Cell team, I brought Jim in to be a part of it. It would only be a 6-month assignment, but very intense.

The job of the team is to plan for the most crazy and impossible scenarios that might arise and how the Agency can deal with them.

In other words, plan and prepare for, "what if," scenarios that nobody else is thinking about and most never even imagine could take place.

This is how you make sure you can respond and deal with anything that comes your way.

Looking over, I could see Angelina slowly fading away, her head nodding at times.

I went over and closed her laptop.

"Come on let's go to bed."

Her eyes opened wide and she looked up at me, gave me a smile and stood up.

I walked her to her room, gave her a kiss on the forehead and said goodnight.

"Good night grandpa."

I smile at her and shut the door.

Chapter 7

The next day was going to be uneventful and I decided to take the girls into town and have brunch. This time we would bring Antonella as well. It was another beautiful sunny day so we had the top down, and all I could see from my peripheral vision was long hair blowing around.

We reached the town, parked, and walked down by the docks so the girls could watch the sail boats before walking up to Sonia's café for brunch.

Sonia and her husband have operated this café for over 30 yrs. They make the most amazing pastries, rolls, and breads.

We sat outside while still enjoying a picturesque view of the bay. We looked over the small menu and were soon greeted by Sonia who took our order. She never had to write anything down, and never made a mistake.

We made small talk as we ate. I sipped coffee as the girls had lemonade. It is so wonderful to see my granddaughter laughing and having so much fun in the place I now call home.

After we finished, I ordered a few loaves of bread and some pastries to take back with us. I put those back in the car, then we strolled along the narrow sidewalk stopping at a store the girls wanted to visit.

I told them they could find one item each and gave them a $25., limit.

After the girls each picked out a gift, I paid the cashier and we walked to the car and headed back home.

While driving the girls made plans to swim, which I agreed to.

I stopped at Franco's home to give Maria a bag of pastries and a loaf of bread, keeping a loaf for myself along with a few pastries, as the girls ran inside to get their bathing suits.

When Italians speak the language very quickly, sometimes it is difficult for me to follow, but I knew Antonella was telling her mother that they were getting their bathing suits and going swimming.

Maria looked at me with an expression as if asking, are you sure it is OK.

"Of course, it's OK, I invited them." I said handing her the bag of baked goods.

"Grazie!."

"You're welcome." I replied

The girls hurried out and back into the car in seconds.

I was already out on the deck with my laptop when the girls came rushing out from Angelina's room ready to swim. One after the other they jumped into the water.

Jim had sent an email confirming that he and his wife would be arriving in Rome the second week of September, and he planned to visit me for a few of those days. That would be perfect because Angelina would be back in the states by then.

I replied to him and let him know which train to take to come visit me, so he could arrange those tickets as well. Since he has never been to Italy, I will arrange to have a friend from the US Embassy in Rome greet him at the airport and show him around. Michael has worked for the US State Department for years and has been a diplomat working in the Rome Embassy for at least 7 yrs. now. Michael helped me a great deal when I moved to Italy, and with acquiring all the necessary documents when purchasing the vineyard, and the transition of the former company over to my company. There is a great deal of licensing, permits, and forms to be filed to operate a vineyard and export wine, and with Michaels knowledge of Italian laws and his diplomatic status, this process moved more quickly than I would have imagined.

I also sent emails to my son and daughter to confirm with them if they could still come spend Christmas here with me, as we discussed some time ago.

It would be the first time all of us would be here in Italy all together. The plan is to have everyone stay for 10 days. This house has six bedrooms, all furnished but most rooms have never been used. Angelina has her own room, which she loves, but she would share it with Giovanna, since there are two beds, and they love whatever time they get to spend together, which is not much due to living so far apart.

Emery and Mark could have a room, and Vincent and Marla have their own room.

Christmas is my favorite time of the year and to have my family with me, all together again, would be amazing. I have already begun planning.

With those few emails sent I went inside to make a jug of sweet, iced tea and returned with several plastic cups for the girls and a big bowl of pretzels.

I placed them on the table. "Girls, there is iced tea and pretzels here if you take a break."

A resounding, "thank you," was heard through the splashing.

I returned to my laptop, opened another email from an old friend. It was an interesting update from a case he and I worked on years ago. It was a case involving the brother of a late drug kingpin, who was the accountant for the Medellin Cartel, a Columbian organized crime syndicate that flooded the US with cocaine back in the 1980's and 1990's. We used our international contacts to assist the FBI with tracking the money trails left behind by this man. They had so much cash coming in that they really did not know what to do with it. It was estimated at the height of their power they earned upwards of $420 million per week. They began making huge payoffs to high level banking executives to launder the cash through their banks, then wired the money to a few thousand fake paper companies set up in the Cayman Islands, which had huge complexes of these paper companies. A paper company would be one room, one employee, a phone and computer, and there were over 12,000 of them.

It was a remarkably interesting yet complicated web of money trails that eventually sent this brother to prison for a long time while his brother the kingpin was shot to death by Colombian police.

The brother who was later released from prison is now in his seventies and had his privacy and location hacked due to a flaw in security updates by Apple to safeguard its products from hackers while exposing a Face Time flaw.

The hackers would begin by calling somebody via Face Time, and before that person picked up the hacker swiped up to add their own phone number to the call.

Once they were added to the call, Face Time immediately treated it like an active conference call, and began sending audio of the person the hacker was calling, even if they had not picked up yet.

Face time videos of this brother began going viral and his locations was revealed.

So, the brother filed a lawsuit against Apple for $2.6 billion.

This is just one reason I am skeptical of video chats, and social media outlets.

I have my home set up with a secure and private internet connection and use a VPN, so I feel a little more comfortable with Angelina using video chats with her girlfriends back home, but have made it clear to her, only answer a video call from a person you know and trust.

But over the years I have taught Angelina, as I have taught my own children, multiple spy defense secrets and combat skills. I want them to know the simple skills and strategies necessary to survive practically any situation you could possibly encounter in the increasingly and chaotic world we live in. This knowledge has changed them at a fundamental level. They are completely different people now. They never enter a room and look at it or the people inside in the same manner. Instead, they now look at the world through the eyes of an operative.

All Intelligence officers develop a," spy sense." It is a complex mix of traits developed through rigorous training, to learn how to survive in the most extreme and dangerous situations imaginable. All intelligence officers have their own special touches they bring to their craft, but ultimately, we all share, "spy sense," as a core foundation. Everyday my children spent time with me was training whether they were aware of it or not. Soon they acquired the 6 must-learn traits that are the core foundation of, spy sense,"

A spy never knows what skills an operation might require, and he must be ready to use everything in his arsenal.

There is no room for error.

The girls were all out of the pool now and having some drinks and sharing the big bowl of pretzels.

I did not have much to eat today and was beginning to get hungry and decided I would go inside and start making dinner.

"I'm going inside to start dinner."

"OK grandpa."

Tonight, I would make a one of our favorites, ravioli.

I am not particularly good in the kitchen at all, but I can manage a few easy meals like this.

I spent most of my life eating every meal at a restaurant, diner, or take-out.

Shortly after, Angelina opened the door, as Antonella and Lucia said goodbye, then she stepped inside.

The girls would just leave the back way and walk down to their home. The Martone's always have an open invitation to use the pool.

Chapter 8

"What's for dinner grandpa?"

"One of our favorite's, ravioli!"

Angelina smiled. "I'm going to change into my PJ's, be right back."

"OK."

By the time she returned I had just dished out the ravioli and was cutting up the fresh loaf of bread.

I enjoyed a glass of wine as she had more iced tea.

"I hope you're not missing home yet?"

"No way! I mean I miss mom and dad and of course my cat, and my friends, but I love this place. And I love spending time with Lucia and Antonella."

"I love having you here."

"Let's watch a movie tonight grandpa!"

"Sure, I will let you find one."

We finished our dinner and Angelina helped me clear the table, as I loaded the dishwasher.

"OK you find a movie; I'm going to put my PJ's on now."

Leaving my bedroom, I made a stop in the kitchen to get a few of the pastries I bought earlier, poured myself another glass of wine and poured a glass of water for Angelina.

"Who wants dessert?'

"I do I do!"

"Help yourself."

She picked a raspberry one while I chose lemon. Sonia makes everything from scratch, and these are amazing.

"Any luck with a movie?"

"Yeah, but not sure you will like it."

"Ha-ha it's OK, I will watch whatever you picked."

"But…."

"But what?" I asked

"How about a story first?"

"Sure. You know where the box is."

She laid down her pastry and went over to the box. This time she lifted out and placed several handfuls of postcards next to the box.

"What are you doing?"

"You have been telling me stories for years and I never go to the bottom."

"There is no need to go to the bottom Angelina, there are plenty we haven't gotten to."

Then she pulled out an old large envelope, closed by a metal clasp. It was an envelope I had not opened in years.

"What's in this grandpa?"

I found myself not breathing as I stared at the envelope.

"Can I open it?"

Memories began to flood my mind, I knew I had not answered her yet, but it seemed like for a moment time had stopped.

"Yes.... yes. You can open it."

I could feel my lungs taking deep breaths. She pulled out several loose postcards.

Then she dumped the envelope out.

I got up and walked over, as she shifted through a half of dozen or so of envelopes, then a few larger blue folders that held 5x7 photos.

"Let's just take one postcard OK." I said as I began stuffing the larger envelopes with the letters and photo folders.

"OK grandpa, how about this one?" holding up a postcard that read, Norwegian Cruise Lines, "The Norway."

"OK." It was one of several. My very first cruise.

We took the postcard and went to the sofa. Angelina turned off the television and took a sip of water while finishing her pastry.

I did the same, sipped my wine, set the glass down. I held the postcard and just stared at it. Angelina snuggled up next to me, and I began to speak.

"I had just turned 23 and graduating with my master's degree. A few of my friends wanted to do something big, something fun and exciting to celebrate. We decided a cruise to the Caribbean would be amazing. So, one of my friends, Bill, had a friend who worked as a travel agent. She began figuring out our best options for the time of the year we would be going.

She narrowed it down to a few options. So, Bill ran the options by Tony and me, and we decided on the cruise ship, The Norway."

"So, you went with two friends, Bill and Tony?"

"Yes."

"The timing of everything was perfect, because I had been approached by a CIA recruiter before graduation, and I had interviews set up just when I would return from the cruise?"

"So, the CIA has recruiters like the military?"

"No. It's not like that. If your major in college lines up with a field they are currently hiring for, they may scout colleges to see if there are any students that may match their criteria. Then they take steps to set up an initial meeting. I can tell you the process another time."

"Yes, no more interruptions, back to the story." She smiled

"So, we went ahead and paid the travel agent for the vacation. It would include roundtrip to Florida, where the cruise began, plus an extra 2 days in Miami after the cruise.

I had never been on a cruise ship like this, so I was extremely excited. The day came, we flew to Miami, took a shuttle arranged by our travel agent, to the cruise ship, and began the process of boarding. It was much warmer and more humid in Florida than back home.

We got on board and trying to find our cabin was like being in a maze. We finally found it and decided which bed we were each taking. I took the single bed, and they took the bunkbed.

We looked over the itinerary for the night and for the entire seven days and nights.

Each night was a different theme, each night had a different after dinner show, it was more than I had imagined.

We left the cabin rather quickly to roam around and find where the lunch buffet was. We passed by the pools and were surprised some people were already swimming.

We found the food at the buffet was delicious and endless."

"I know you loved that grandpa."

"Oh yes. So, we ate and just watched all the people. It was getting more crowded as time went on.

Eventually we made our way back to the cabin to get dressed for the evening. We had arranged for the later dinner seating.

We found our dining room and a very friendly host showed us to our table. We were seated with three other people to complete a round table of six. Each night we would have the same table, and same people. Remember, me and my friends were 23. The other three were a married couple maybe in their mid to late 50's and the woman's father who had to be mid-seventies. The point, it was not an overly exciting table, but nonetheless we shared many laughs over the next 7 dinners.

After dinner that first night, we went to the show, it was a very well-done play. Everything so far was top notch. Servers even took our drink orders as we sat watching the play.

Afterwards, we roamed around. It was dark, but the ship was lit up like a circus, lights everywhere. If you got close to the railings you could hear the waves splashing against the massive ship as we moved swiftly to our first destination.

We decided to go to one of the dance clubs. It was crowded and I am sure most were not of legal drinking age, but that law seemed a little relaxed.

I was not looking to meet a girl. I had recently ended a relationship that lasted a few years. But I was not opposed to talking to a girl and soon enough my friends and I sparked up a conversation with two girls who seemed to be flirting with most of the guys.

They were friends and from California, Ciara and Kim, on vacation with their parents. Turns out they had just graduated high school, but the bartender kept serving them drinks regardless.

We could tell they were party girls, well it seemed Kim really was, and Ciara just tagged along. Bill liked to dance and soon he was up at the dance floor with the two girls, as Tony and I just sat and took in the club.

It was not long before they ditched Bill and left with a few guys. We stayed a bit longer, finished our drinks, then roamed around the enormous ship until the midnight buffet began."

"They have a buffet at midnight?"

"Yes. And the food is always amazing. Cruises have the best chefs. But before the buffet we had time to explore, stopping at several other small quiet clubs. One had a jazz band, and another a solo piano player. Mostly older people visited those bars. During our journey, we saw that girl Kim from the club emerge from a room, carrying her shoes, and appeared to be very drunk. Then a guy's head peaked out and yelled to her that he will see her tomorrow."

Thankfully, I do not think Angelina understood what I was alluding to.

"Finally, we arrived at the dining room where the buffet was just about to begin. We ate until we could hardly move. Then we made our way back to the cabin, using the map given to us when we boarded to find our way.

It was late, or rather early in the morning, we all had a long tiring day, and passed out quickly, only to awake to the alarm clock just hours later at 8am."

"Let me guess, breakfast buffet?" Angelina asked as she laughed.

"Yes! Then we went to one of the pools, there were two. It was difficult to find chairs, but we managed to get 3 together. The sun was extremely hot, but the constant breeze made it feel wonderful.

We took a walk over to the other side of the ship, to the second pool, it was just as crowded. We had a server bring us a few drinks and sipped on them as we walked back to our chairs.

There really was not a lot going on. Sure, there was a gym, and basketball, and other activities, but most were crowded, and besides this was vacation. I wanted to eat, drink, get tan, and have fun.

Today we just sailed, tomorrow we would stop at the first Island."

"So cool."

"Yes, each one incredibly beautiful. Our ship stopped at one Island each day for the next five days.

Pretty much every night was the same. Have an amazing dinner, go to a show, then stroll around, stopping at the dance club, and a few quieter places.

And every night the dinner menu was different. I am sure most people around us thought we were traveling with our grandparents. We had the quietest table, but a crazy waiter who kept things alive, and brought us all the food we could eat.

During the show, that second night, Bill happened to notice that California girl Kim sitting with and kissing a different guy, as her poor friend just sat there watching the show. It was pretty obvious she wasn't guy crazy."

"Were they both pretty grandpa?"

"Yes, very pretty, actually Ciara was much prettier. And because she was not seeking so much attention from all the guys, it made her even more beautiful.

We just laughed and ordered a few drinks."

30

"What was the show that night?

"It was a musical, incredibly good. The cast were top notch. Afterwards we stopped at the dance club. We sat near a few girls and soon struck up a conversation. They were all from Ohio, and like us had just graduated college.

Ciara and Kim were already there. Shortly after, Ciara made her way over to me and asked if I would dance with Kim. She told me Kim thought I was cute."

"Grandpa." Smirked Angelina.

"Remember, she found every guy cute. I had already seen her dancing with two different guys, so my number was up."

Angelina laughed.

"So, we danced and made small talk. Tony came along and asked Ciara to dance, so we four danced a few songs."

"I can't picture you dancing grandpa."

"Me either. I'm awful. I could tell Kim had already had a lot to drink. Who even knew where her parents were hiding to allow there eighteen-year-old daughter to get so intoxicated and be with so many men?

The song ended and Tony and I headed back over to our table. Bill was out dancing with the Ohio girls. When he returned to the table, we had one more drink then left and walked around, making sure to cover the entire ship, before making our way to the midnight buffet. At night, you could see nothing but the moonlight shinning across the massive ocean."

I could sense Angelina was growing a bit tired. Swimming for a few hours and me going on and on with this long story had her ready for bed. There would be no movie tonight.

"Hey, let's head to bed Angel, it's been a long day."

"But the story isn't over."

"It's a long story, lets continue tomorrow night OK."

"K."

I walked her to her room and kissed her forehead.

"Good night my little angel."

"Night grandpa."

Chapter 9

The next morning as I was having coffee, Maria called and asked if Angelina would like to drive into town to shop at the markets for groceries. I assured her Angelina would love that.

"Angelina!"

"Yes grandpa?" She answered walking out of her room.

"Have some breakfast, Mrs. Martone is picking you up in 30 minutes to go grocery shopping in town. Antonella and Lucia are both going as well."

Her eyes lit up, "Great!"

So, she sat with me and we had some cereal.

"Grandpa, I really like this story. I mean, it is before you even met grandma and before my dad was even born. You have told me so many work-related stories over the years, but this is the first story of your life, before you were even married. It's really cool."

I just smiled. "I'm glad you like it; we'll continue it tonight."

I stared into my coffee cup as memories from that cruise flashed through my mind. This story is not just an ordinary vacation related story. This story is much deeper and more meaningful. It is a story that, even to this day, frequents my thoughts.

I could hear the Martone's car pulling up and within moments there was a knock at the door. Angelina and I were both watching the small monitor in the kitchen that captures images from several cameras surrounding my home, so we knew it was Lucia.

"Coming!" Angelina shouted as she scooted away from the table and put her tennis shoes on.

I got up and opened the door.

The girls were so excited to be hanging out again together.

I waved to Maria and thanked her for including Angelina, then kissed Angelina on the forehead and handed her some money to put in her pocket in case she needed it for a snack or a drink.

I watched the car slowly drive down the long driveway, then walked backed to the kitchen table to finish my breakfast. As the car waited for the gates to open, I watched Angelina and Lucia laughing in the back seat, oblivious to the inconspicuous concealed camera aimed at the gates watching them.

I stared over at the box that holds the post cards and memories. In my mind I was unsure if I wanted to go down this road.

Angelina found those postcards and envelopes that I had purposely kept on the bottom of the pile. They contained memories of, "what ifs," and "what could have been."

I got up and walked over to the box, opened it and took out one of the larger envelopes. Inside, were several photos from that very cruise.

Throughout my life I have been on many cruises, but they all left me with an emptiness. They could never compare to the experience I had on that very first cruise.

I had not opened this envelope in years, but I had to. I looked at each photo carefully, paying attention to every detail contained in each one. It became a bit overwhelming and I put the photos back in and clasped it shut with the metal tab.

I went to refill my coffee and make my way into the office to get some work done.

It was hard to concentrate as old memories now swarmed through my head. I went back to the box and took out a different envelope, that contained letters.

I reached in and randomly chose one and slid it out. Her handwriting was unique, beautiful, and enthusiastic. I found myself smiling as I read and hung onto every word. It was so strange to see it addressed to my childhood home, where I was still living at that point in time.

This envelope contained a three-page handwritten letter. Everything was handwritten back then, and this, like her other letters, was written in her signature neon pink ink pen.

I left the envelope and walked back to my office, carrying the pages whiles reading. I sat down and continued. I soaked in every word, every detail she emphasized. Each word began to bring me back to that place and time. She had just begun working part time at a hometown local shoe store to earn some money while she attended her first semester of college. For me, I was officially hired by the agency after a few months of interviews and vigorous testing. The five-year difference in our age meant nothing. We were connected on every level. She mentioned several times how much she missed me and wanted me to come and visit her. Unfortunately, I would not be able to visit her. My extensive training would be starting soon, and I was not allowed to tell anyone, even my family and friends. I had to come up with a fabricated story of how I landed a decent job at an accounting firm in Virginia, which was now my new home. I no longer used actual residential addresses, from now on it was post office boxes and mail drops.

After pausing and reflecting throughout the entire letter I had finally made it to the end and noticed almost an hour had passed.

I folded the letter very carefully using the exact same crease and inserted it back into the envelope, imagining her beautiful hands touching this same paper so many years ago. I picked up the cup of coffee, which was now cold, and slowly spun my chair to face the window. Gazing out across the beautiful green hills of Bardolino, I could not help but to think, "what if."

Chapter 10

It has been just over two hours and I figured Maria and the girls would be here soon.

In these small towns they do not have huge grocery store chains as they do in America. There are many little stores, some specializing in different things.

In America we dread grocery shopping and race around filling up a large cart then race to the checkout, cutting off people along the way in the hopes of getting the last self-checkout machine and avoid human contact. I get it, I was that way.

But here, shopping is an experience. Everybody knows each other. The shop owners know their customers and what they like. They talk, ask about relatives, it is a true community.

I took this time to make several business-related phone calls. It was nice to get these things out of the way without distracting my time away from Angelina.

Soon I saw Maria pull up to the gate. Only several people have the passcode to the gate besides myself, which include Franco, Maria, and Salvatore, their oldest son.

From my office I can scan most of the entire property thanks to the strategically placed cameras I had installed. I walked out onto the front porch as the car approached. Angelina got out waving goodbye to the girls as I waved and thanked Maria again.

I placed my hand on Angelina's shoulder as we walked inside and I asked her if she had fun, her smile answered my question.

"It was so much fun!"

"Grandpa, I'm going to call my parents and then chat with my friends before we eat OK."

"Sure, tell your mom and dad I said hello."

I finished up a few more things in the office. Then I walked down the hall, past Angelina's room to go to my bedroom. I heard her vibrant voice, go to a whisper.

My curiosity had me walk back and stand quietly outside her door just to make sure she was not upset about anything and did not want to tell me.

"I just think grandpa is lonely, he must be. He has this big house, all this land, and he's all alone."

"No, he didn't tell me that, but he must be."

I assumed she was speaking with her mother, and her thoughtfulness made me smile. She always assumes I must be lonely, and she is always trying to find a pretty woman in town that she feels would be a good girlfriend for me.

I then continued to my room to change into shorts and T-shirt and made my way to the basement, shouting to Angelina that I would be exercising.

Ever since I was a teenager, I have enjoyed working out to keep in shape, so I converted a third of the basement into a basic home gym consisting of everything I needed for a good workout.

When I finished and went back upstairs, I could now hear Angelina chatting with her friends.

I went into my bedroom, showered and got dressed, then headed to the kitchen to begin making an early dinner.

Chapter 11

During dinner we talked about the day and she told me all about how fun the shopping was.

"Grandpa I cannot wait for the rest of that story! I've been waiting all day."

"Ha Ha Ok we will finish it. Let us finish this first and I may have some cookies for dessert."

"Perfect!"

She helped me clear the table, as I loaded the dishwasher. She poured herself another glass of lemonade and I poured a glass of wine. She went to the table the box was on and picked up the postcard from last night, as I got a small box of cookies from a cabinet, then we met on the sofa.

"Here you go." She said handing me the card.

Then she picked out a few cookies and leaned back into me. We were both comfortable, and I took a sip of wine as she nibbled on a cookie.

"Let's see, where did I leave off? Oh yes, the third day. Well we went to a beautiful island and instead of doing what most tourists did, we decided to take a taxi and go to a private beach we had heard about. Which, looking back was a bit crazy because we could have been robbed, but it turned out to be a great time.

Then after going back to the ship, we all took showers and got ready for another eventful evening. We were starving because we didn't eat much all day except for a quick breakfast at the ships buffet and a chicken sandwich from a little tiki grill on the beach.

We each ordered 2 meals at dinner, then left very full as we made our way to the theater."

"What was the show that night?"

"An illusionist, and he was very good."

"And did you see the girl who was boy crazy?" She asked rolling her eyes.

I burst out laughing at her question.

"Yes, as we were leaving, we saw Ciara and Kim in a back row, Kim kissing a different guy of course, as Ciara just sat there, her eyes almost asking us to take her away, as we all waved to her. Even she seemed tired of her friend's promiscuous behavior."

"Promiscuous?" Angelina asked.

"It means immoral behavior."

"Kim looked at me and I just shook my head and smirked. She knew at that point I was not going to be just another number.

So, my friends and I left and just walked. I was in the mood for a quiet piano bar for our first stop, Bill and Tony agreed.

Bill was the navigation expert, always having the map of the ship handy. He led us into the other dining rooms lobby area to find an elevator to take us up to the deck where one of the piano bars were located.

There were two young ladies waiting for the elevator and we stood behind them. They each had beautiful long hair and exotic tans.

As they conversed amongst each other I could not but help notice the most beautiful accents and sweetest voices ever. Growing up in New York I have never heard such accents.

The doors opened and we stepped in after the young ladies. They then turned around to face the strangers aboard the elevator with them.

They were both gorgeous, a little shy, yet without hesitation they said, *how ya'll doing*?

They were so friendly and so sweet, I had to ask where they were from with such beautiful accents.

We are doing good, I responded. Then I said, you two have the most beautiful accents. Where are you from?

The one that really caught my eye said, we are from Oklahoma.

I have never met anyone from Oklahoma, neither has Tony or Bill. But Tony and Bill did not seem as captivated as I was. We each introduced ourselves. Their names were Keri and Tonia. The girls kiddingly did not acknowledge their accents but told us we had the accents. They asked where we were from. I told them New York. Likewise, they have never met anyone from New York.

Moments later the elevator door opened, and we all got out. I somehow convinced the two girls to come with us to the piano bar.

Now, since men are very visual, I immediately knew I was attracted to Keri.

We slowly walked the deck being led by our guide Bill."

Giving Angelina a little squeeze we both laughed at that remark.

"The deck was quite busy as we walked and talked until Bill told us we were there. We went in and found a booth in the rear of the bar. The booth was shaped like a semi-circle and I took one end with Keri next to me, Tonia next to her, then Tony and Bill. We ordered drinks and I was surprised the girls even ordered alcoholic beverages called pina colodas."

"I think my mom likes those," Angelina remarked.

"I'm sure she does, they are very good." I responded with a laugh.

"This particular evening had a formal dinner attire code, so basically the men wore suits and ties, and the ladies wore formal dresses. And Keri and Tonia knocked it out of the park. They wore the most beautiful dresses. Their hair was perfectly styled, each with just a touch of make up to accent their natural youthful beauty.

As we waited for the drinks, I asked the girls how old they were. Keri told us they were 18. Surprisingly, the slight age difference did not seem to faze any of us guys. Then she asked how old we were, and I told her we were all 23. And by her smile I could tell it did not faze them either.

The piano bar was much more relaxing and quieter than the night club, so we were able to carry on a conversation without screaming.

The man playing the piano was exceptionally good, accompanied by an excellent female singer. Several couples were slow dancing and I asked Keri if she would like to dance if I promised not to step on her feet."

Angelina and I laughed.

"Did she say yes grandpa?"

"She did. So, we went up to dance. Soon, Tony and Tonia came up to dance as well.

When the song ended, we went back to the table and finished our drinks. Bill suggested we go to the night club. But my idea was to get to know Keri a little more. I didn't want to separate her from her friend, but I wasn't opposed to suggesting a thought in the hopes of persuading her to stay with me for one more drink then we would meet the three of them at the night club.

It went as planned which told me that Keri may have been interested in me as well.

We joked about her and Tonia ordering drinks since they were not of legal drinking age, as I ordered us another drink and we became fully immersed in each other. With every word she spoke, her beautiful, sweet accent drew me in deeper. She had long wavy brown hair with streaks of blonde blended in thanks to the sun I assumed, and such an amazing dark tan. Her perfect white teeth seemed to glow against her tan skin in the dimly lit atmosphere. At the time I could not tell if her eyes were blue or green, they were unique and seemed to change with the lighting. She was the most beautiful girl I had ever seen.

We finished our drinks and decided to leave the bar and reunite with our friends at the night club. It was the last place I wanted to be, but it was not right to leave Tonia with two strange guys and without her girlfriend.

I had already felt such a deep connection with this girl, and I knew we only had three days and nights left. I did not want to waste time trying to meet other girls, Keri was the only one I was interested in, and I was beginning to feel she felt the same way.

As we slowly walked, I asked her if I could hold her hand. She smiled, and with no words, or missing a step, our hands joined."

I can still remember how soft and silky her hand was. Her nails were trimmed perfectly and painted a light pink.

"As we navigated in the direction of the night club, we found a little area with a few comfortable looking lounge chairs overlooking the water and beautiful clear sky full of stars. She suggested we sit for a few minutes and just take in this breathtaking view. I pulled two lounge chairs together as we continued to learn more about each other. The breeze was cool, and I could see she seemed a bit cold, so I stood up, took off my suit jacket and laid it over her like a blanket.

I reached for her hand once again. Minutes turned into hours and we realized the deck was now empty, nobody standing or walking, just the silence of the night and the faint sound of waves crashing off the ship. She checked her watch, and it was 1:25am.

We got up and made our way to the night club. By the time we got there Tony, Tonia, and Bill were gone.

So, I walked her to her room, which she shared with Tonia. They were both there with their parents and had three rooms reserved, all next to each other. Her parents and little brother in one room, Tonia's parents in another, and luckily, the girls had their own room because they sort of had a midnight curfew.

Keri asked me to wait outside while she went in to see if Tonia was there. I was relieved to hear them talking. Keri then came back out, and said Tonia was so worried when we never showed up at the club, and that Tony and Bill walked her back to the room and assured her that I was a good guy and she had no need to worry.

Keri's parents were right next door, hopefully asleep, so she gave me back my jacket, we hugged, and said goodnight, but not before making plans to find each other the next day."

As I walked away from her cabin, I found myself already missing her. I hoped she did not turn out to be like that other girl from California, just looking to score with any guy who gave her attention. I was always able to read people well, ever since I was young, and I did not get that vibe at all from Keri.

"Luckily, I had a map of the ship in my jacket pocket, so I was able to navigate my way back to my cabin. I only passed several people, and we were on the opposite side of the ship.

Tony and Bill were sleeping when I got there. So, I quickly changed into shorts and T-shirt and went to bed. We had to wake up early in order to eat a quick breakfast and then get in line to take a tender to the island."

"What's a tender?"

"It's a smaller ship that takes passenger to and from the island docks because our ship was too big and had to anchor a distance away."

I laid in bed and stared at the ceiling. My mind replayed the events of the evening as I felt the gentle motion of the ship making its way through the water. I could not stop thinking of Keri.

"What do you say we end it here tonight and pick it back up tomorrow night OK.?

"But grandpa it's so interesting."

"Really?"

"Yes, I love it. It's such a good story."

"OK we will pick it back up tomorrow. We need to get some rest."

I promised my son I would keep Angelina on a schedule she is used to, and with the 6-hour time difference it takes time to get adjusted, although Angelina has not seemed to be thrown off at all.

I walked her to her room, gave her a kiss on her forehead and we said goodnight.

Chapter 12

The next morning, I woke up and made my way to the kitchen to make coffee before working out.

To my surprise Angelina was already awake and sitting at the smaller dining room table that we eat at.

"Good morning grandpa."

"Good morning kiddo you're up early?

As I was making coffee I glanced over and noticed the large envelope which contained the photos from that cruise.

"Grandpa, come here, is this Keri with you?"

She had several photos spread out on the table but was holding up one of my favorites.

I walked over and smiled down at her.

"Yes, that's her."

"Grandpa she is so beautiful."

"She sure was."

"And you were so young grandpa."

"Hey…. I'm still young, just not as young." I said laughing.

Angelina did not take her eyes off the photo during this exchange, but she did manage to laugh at my remark about being young.

"Was this at one of the islands grandpa?"

"Yes, I will tell you tonight during our story time OK."

"And these other pictures to ok?"

"Yes, I will tell you when and where they were taken tonight. Right now, I need some coffee and I'm going downstairs to exercise."

"Can Lucia and I ride the bikes today?"

"Sure!"

Chapter 13

When I came back upstairs after my workout, Angelina was still sitting at the table, the photos still spread out as she was watching a video on her laptop.

"I'm so hungry grandpa, are you ready for breakfast?"

"Yes, why don't you put the photos back in the envelope and I will bring breakfast over."

As I brought over milk and cereal Angelina took the envelope over and laid it upon the lid of the closed box of memories. She left all the photos from that cruise on top of the envelope.

It has been years since I have taken those photo's out. Although very distant memories, they always remained significant to me.

"I have a surprise weekend set up for us."

"Really?" Angelina's eyes lit up.

"Yes. We leave in the morning."

"Where to? What do you have planned?"

"We are going into town and taking a boat to a beautiful town called, Sirmione. We are staying two nights at a spa complex called Virgillo & Catullo."

"A spa?" She exclaimed; her eyes so big.

"Yes. It is an extremely popular place, with numerous restaurants, fashion stores, hotels, and a large outdoor market area. It will be so fun."

"OMG it sounds so awesome grandpa."

"We will have a great time. So, pack a few things tonight for two days."

We finished breakfast and Angelina went to meet up with Lucia. They loved riding the bikes all around the vineyard, and Lucia would get to see her father and brothers working.

While in Sirmione, an old friend from the agency will be meeting me for dinner.

He is a cryptologist and has been working in Rome.

We recruited him out of the Defense Intelligence Agency (DIA), where he was a naval officer.

His first assignment was in Afghanistan, and I was the Chief of the station, the officer in charge at the time. Until then his only intelligence experience was behind guarded walls and offices of government facilities in the US. Now he was entering a warzone.

After the 9/11 attacks and the US invaded Afghanistan, we set up surveillance facilities throughout that country to continue fighting and protect US interest.

Afghanistan is not a vacation resort as David soon found out. It is extremely hot and overpopulated. The whole country is smaller than the state of Texas but has over 9 million more residents. It was a haven for terrorist groups like al Qaeda and riddled with poverty, child malnutrition, and corruption.

I needed someone there with David's knowledge and expertise to work with our interpreters. It proved to be beneficial, and we were able to pinpoint a few locations and take out several mid to high level terrorists who were plotting against us and our allies in the middle east.

I have not seen David in years and was looking forward to catching up at dinner. But I knew there was a deeper meaning for this dinner/meeting. One is never truly retired from the agency if your knowledge and experience are still a commodity.

Chapter 14

I took this time to get some work done in the office. I was looking forward to this little trip to Sirmione and had planned it several weeks ago.

The general manager has become a friend since I bought the vineyard. My wines are exceedingly popular amongst guests at the hotels and restaurants there and I always make sure they never run short. People come from all over the world to visit this little oasis nestled along the lake of this ancient, fortified town.

After several hours of phone calls and emails, I walked out onto the porch to see if I could see the girls. From a distance I could see them casually making their way through the winding roads of the vineyard and heading in this direction.

I walked back inside, the went over to where Angelina had left the photos. I picked them up, and as I viewed each photo, I revisited the exact memory of it. I found myself smiling, wondering what Keri was doing at that very moment.

Years ago, I asked my assistant to do a little searching for Keri, to see if she was married and where she was living.

I simply provided a name and the town where she lived when I knew her. My assistant, or handler as we call them, was incredibly good at her job. Handler's assist officers by providing anything needed and using the full scope of the agency's resources and networks to do so effectively and efficiently. This simple task was completed within minutes. I can still remember the feeling I got when she told me Keri had been married and still living in Oklahoma. She handed me a piece of paper that had the information, the church, the pastors name, the date, her last known job and current address. Years of the unknown was now in my hand and I still was not ready to accept it, even though I was married myself at that time.

I wondered now, if she was still married, if she had children, if she has grandchildren, is she still alive and healthy and if so, does she still live in Oklahoma, what work did she pursue in life, was she happy, and did she ever think about me.

Suddenly this time of reflection was interrupted by a door slamming and my granddaughter yelling how thirsty she was.

"You know where the refrigerator is." I responded as I laid the photos back down.

As Angelina poured herself a glass of lemonade she asked if I wanted some.

"Sure." I responded, sliding my glass her way.

"How was the bike ride?"

"So fun. We saw her brothers and father. I just love it here grandpa."

"I'm glad to hear that. Maybe we can convince your parents to let you spend every summer here."

"That would be so awesome!" She said with a big smile.

"Why don't we pack, have an early dinner, and get a good night sleep for our little trip."

"OK., and don't forget I want to hear more about the story and Keri."

"Sounds good."

47

Chapter 15

After dinner Angelina helped clear the dishes as usual and I brought a plate of cookies to lay on the table besides the sofa we like to sit on.

Angelina stopped to get the photos before coming over to sit next to me.

"So where was this photo taken?"

"This was taken by a cruise ship photographer as we were walking out of the ocean at the private island owned by the cruise line."

"They own an island?"

"Yes, it's a small island and they bring a lot of food over from the ship and have a big cookout for all the quests. We had met Keri and Tonia there. Keri had rented one of those body boards so she could float around. She asked if I wanted to join her, so I did. We went out until the water was maybe 10-feet-deep and just held onto the board and talked for hours, occasionally diving and swimming to the bottom and back up. The water was crystal clear and warm as a bath. We had such an amazing connection. It's like we were never lost for words or things to talk about. Eventually we decided to swim back to land and get something to eat and meet up with our friends that we seemed to have forgotten about. And that is when that picture was taken. The photographer was ankle deep in the water and taking photos of the passengers. Then later, the photos would be on display in a large gallery on the ship, and you can find your photo and of course purchase it."

"She is so beautiful grandpa."

I smiled, as we both stared at the photo. We were so young. Keri's long hair was wet and slicked back from a simple motion of plugging her nose and dipping her head backwards into the water, so all her hair was away from her face and down her back. That photo of her still takes my breath.

"You two look like a perfect couple grandpa."

I cracked a smile and nodded my head in agreement.

Then Angelina put that photo aside and held up another photo. This was the second and final professional photo taken of Keri and I on that cruise. The other few photos are ones that either Tony or Tonia took.

"This was taken as we left the theater after watching a play. All of us sat together during this show, with Keri being next to me, Tonia next to her, then Bill and Tony."

"That pirate guy is being silly grandpa." Angelina said as she laughed.

There was a guy in a pirate costume outside the doors of the theater taking photos as we exited. He thought it was funny to point his plastic sword towards my groin area, which had Keri and I cracking up laughing while the photographer took the photo.

"He sure was." I replied.

"And guess what the play was that evening?"

"What?" Asked Angelina.

"Oklahoma, a musical, and that's where Keri and Tonia lived."

"That is so funny." Angelina replied in laughter.

"That night we all went to the dance club, but it was clear Keri, and I were off in our own little world, laughing, dancing, and yes.... drinking. After several hours, we all decided we were a little hungry, so we made our way to the midnight buffet. We got there a little early but were allowed inside to get a drink. They had every juice you could think of, flavored iced teas, lemonade, and a soda machine. Once the buffet tables were opened, we each made a plate of food and found an empty table away from others. We all made conversation as we picked at our plates. Of course, the guys went up for seconds...maybe thirds."

"Of course." Angelina commented.

"Tony and Bill agreed to walk Tonia back to her room, while Keri and I walked and walked until finding comfortable seats again along the ships deck. We held hands the entire time. Cruises can be so romantic, and I was happy to spend these moments with Keri. She was so interesting to me. We were more comfortable with each other now, and she decided to join me in my lounge chair."

Like it was yesterday I remember her asking if there was room for her next to me. I moved over a bit and told her of course. Her red dress looked gorgeous against her beautiful tan skin. She slipped off her sandals and laid next to me. Her toenails were painted a deep red which accented her dress so beautifully. She was the most stylish and fashionable girl I had ever met.

"And I put my arm around her just like this." I said, giving Angelina a gentle squeeze with my arm that was already around her. She laughed.

Keri's body molded right into mine, a perfect fit. I closed my eyes and paused the story. Suddenly I was back in that moment. I still faintly remember the smell of her perfume as I leaned my head into hers. A red ribbon kept most of her hair up on top of her head, so her ears were visible. We did not speak. Both of us just adjusting to this closeness we had not experienced with each other yet. Under some circumstances first time moments like this could be awkward. You are never sure exactly what thoughts or feelings are running through the others mind. But there was no awkwardness, no hesitation. I placed a soft kiss on Keri's ear. I remember feeling a steady increase in my breathing. I then placed a soft kiss on her neck. Her gold hoop earring reflected the moons glowing shine, as I kissed her neck again. It's almost as if the sound of the waves crashing against the ship so far below us had diminished. I could only hear her breathing softly.

As a guy, making this first intention, can be very risky. There is a fear the girl will reject you and declare she just wishes to be friends. It is a true test of confidence without trying to offend the girl. Any fears of rejection were suddenly cast aside as Keri slowly turned her head and placed her velvety soft lips against mine. Our eyes locked and without a word or even a nod, I was assured we were in the exact same moment. We continued to kiss for a long time, breaking every so often to kiss each other's neck or ears. I was lost in her. Nothing else seemed to exist or matter at that time.

"Then what grandpa? Did you kiss?"

"So, we laid together for a while, watching the stars, and yes we did kiss a few times."

Angelina thought that was funny and giggled.

"Then we decided we needed to get some sleep and enjoy the next day. It would be the last full day and night sailing before arriving back in Miami Florida the following morning. So, we walked back to her room and this time I gave her a good night kiss, and we made plans to meet at the pool after breakfast."

I remember walking back to my cabin, the decks were pretty much empty except for a few employees cleaning or straightening things up. There was an emptiness inside me, a sadness, that I may never see Keri again after this cruise. I could not tell her of my future plans with the agency, or where I was even going to be living if I was indeed hired. The recruiter made it clear to not tell anyone, not even family members.

"By the time I got inside our cabin Tony and Bill were asleep. I changed into my PJs and fell asleep quickly. I knew the alarm Bill set everyday would be screaming at 8am, which only gave me a few hours to sleep.

A few hours seemed like mere minutes when I woke to the blaring alarm. We all stumbled out of bed, got dressed, and headed to the dining room. We decided to enjoy a relaxing sit-down breakfast for our last day and be waited on instead of just grabbing things at the breakfast buffet and wandering around trying to find an empty table outside.

After breakfast, I went to the gym to workout. It was not too crowded, and I was able to use what free weights I needed as an aerobics class was going on in the background.

Suddenly I heard a knock on the large glass panel behind me. It was Keri and Tonia walking by and happen to notice me."

Keri was standing there, a big smile, cute shorts and white shirt, holding her flip flops in her left hand and waving to me with her right. I smiled and waved back, motioning for them to meet me at the door.

"And this picture," I said while pointing to it as it laid on the blanket covering Angelina's legs, "was taken right there at the gym by Tonia."

"They were headed to the pool, so I cut my workout short and went with them. We located Tony and Bill, who luckily saved three chairs for us, since the decks were filling up fast. Keri and I went for a swim. We wanted to enjoy as much time alone as possible."

"And is this picture of you and her in the pool that day?" Asked Angelina, as she held up a photo Tony took of us standing in the water.

"Yes!"

"So, we all enjoyed the day and talked about how we didn't want this cruise to end. Keri and I took little escapes into the pool, even though the pool was quite crowded, we were away from our friends and could just enjoy each other without worrying about spending precious time talking to people we see all the time. I know it sounds rude, but this was my last full day with Keri."

"I get it grandpa."

"Then Keri told me she wanted me to meet her parents that evening during dinner. I was a bit hesitant because she was just 18 and I was 23."

"Five years is not that big of a deal grandpa."

"I know." I smirked. I love this little girl.

"I told Keri of course I would meet them."

To me, this was a big move. It showed me that I meant more to her than just a guy she met on vacation.

"She wanted me to come over to her dining room, which was just the opposite side of mine, right before dessert would be served, and have dessert with them. She would meet me at the entrance, and we would walk over to their table together. It wouldn't just be her parents, Tonia's parents would be there as well, and of course Keri's younger brother."

"After spending the whole day at the pool, eating lunch together, swimming, having so much fun, we all decided it was time to go back to our cabins and get ready for our last dinner and evening. I took a nap while Tony and Bill showered and got dressed. They woke me when they were done and told me they would meet me at the bar just outside the dining room. This worked out perfectly because I had the cabin to myself for once. So, I showered, shaved, put on a nice pair of pants and my favorite shirt. I wanted to look my best for Keri, and try to make a good impression on her parents, which isn't always easy." I laughed.

"Just ask your aunt Emery about some of the guys she brought home to meet me and your grandmother." I said rolling my eyes as Angelina cracked up laughing.

"What about these last two pictures grandpa?"

"Let's not jump ahead, I will get to them."

"After all the dinner plates were cleared, I excused myself. I had already told Tony and Bill I was going to meet Keri's parents. I found myself becoming a little nervous as I made my way across the large hallway and entering the other dining room. Keri must have been watching for me as within seconds of me scanning the room I caught a glimpse of her walking towards me. She looked absolutely stunning. She had her hair fixed in a way I have not yet seen it, wavy and flowing across her shoulders and halfway down her back. I just wanted to hug and kiss her, but I could see her entire table staring at us in the distance. She took my hand and led me over to the table of glaring eyes." I laughed.

That comment made Angelina laugh as well.

"One by one she introduced me to each person. I shook hands with the four parents. They welcomed me and invited me to sit down and join them for dessert. An extra chair was already situated next to Keri, as her and I sat at the same time. It only took a few seconds before the questions began being fired my way"

"Ha ha ha, that's funny grandpa."

"Not when you are the one having the questions fired upon." I laughed back

"I made it through the questioning and managed to eat dessert before we excused ourselves to go meet my friends for the last show. I felt things went really well and as soon as we left the room both Keri and Tonia assured me it went very well, and they could tell their parents all seemed to like me."

This was a huge relief for me.

"I would never see Keri's parents again, but it was important for me to make a good first impression, not only for myself, but for the respect I had for Keri."

I wanted to make that clear to Angelina, so she would know how important respect was, and for her to always expect that level of respect from any guy she may date in the future.

"We met up with the guys at the theater. They were both smiling and asked how it went with the parents. As men, we know it can be a difficult task to win over parents. The girls assured them it went well and I agreed. We sat and ordered some drinks. Keri took my hand, leaned in and kissed me. She thanked me for meeting her parents. I told her it was a pleasure."

As Keri crossed her legs, I could not help but look down and admire her beautiful tan. She was wearing a white skirt and a beautiful black shirt with very sexy black strappy sandals. When my eyes looked back up to meet hers, she was smiling and asked if I liked what I saw. She asked it in such a cute but seductive way, it made me smile, and I remember telling her I loved what I saw, to which she kissed me again.

"What was the show that night grandpa?"

"For the last show they did a medley of several different popular plays that most people would know. It was really good. The performers were amazing as usual."

The truth is, the show was not my focus that evening, it was more of a background to a much more meaningful real-life show transpiring between Keri and I. We did not need to speak, just holding hands, looking at each other in the darkness of the theater, something magical was happening and we both felt it.

"When the show ended Keri whispered to Tonia that she wanted to spend this last night with me. I heard her apologize to Tonia, but her friend was very understanding. Once again, my friends stepped up and invited Tonia to go to the dance club with them, which she did, I think Tony liked Tonia, but it never went anywhere.

Keri and I took one last moonlight walk. Those last two pictures were taken with her camera. We asked a woman to take a photo of us. She suggested a few different poses, and this is what came out."

The quality isn't great. Those disposable cameras back then had poor quality but captured a moment none the less.

"You two look so happy grandpa. You both have such beautiful smiles and white teeth."

I laughed.

"We were happy. It was sad when the cruise ended, but at least I got to spend most of the cruise with her.

Since it was still quite early and the guys were at the club with Tonia, I suggested that we go to my cabin and see if anything good was on the television, so we could have a little quiet time while laying next to each other without the confinements of a lounge chair."

Sometimes Angelina gets so caught up in one of my stories she doesn't pick up on some of the more subtle things I happen to say, from an adults perspective, and I have to be very careful to never let anything slip especially any implications consisting of sexual nature, assassinations, classified information, or secrets.

Keri and I both wanted time alone, not in a crowded pool, ocean, theater, or with friends and strangers. I wanted to lay next to her and hold her, kiss her, and just enjoy each other.

"Back then they didn't have all the sources and options for internet connections, so we had to settle for just a few channels that came in through the ships network."

"Were you able to find a movie or anything good to watch?"

"You know what, I think one channel came in clear, but it was nothing we found entertaining,

"We decided to go back out and find one of the quiet piano bars."

"Where were her parents and little brother? You don't really mention them."

"Her parents just hung out with Tonia's parents I guess, maybe went to the casino, or bingo. And the little brother was part of the youth program so every evening after dinner they had events planned and coordinated by youth counselors."

"Sounds so cool. I want to go on a cruise now!"

"I will put a little bug in your father's ear OK."

"Please do!"

In reality, we did not leave the room that soon. We did not seem to mind that nothing good was on television, or that I did not even have anything to offer her since we had no drinks or snacks other than perhaps some bottles of water and chewing gum.

I turned off the light and walked over to her as she sat on the edge of my bed. Our cabin had a porthole, and the moon gave us just enough light to see each other.

Everything about Keri turned me on. As I reached her, she was looking up at me and I down at her. I bent down to kiss her lips. I then kneeled before her, our eyes now meeting just inches apart. It was the same feeling every time our eyes met. It was like the world stopped all around us and she was my only focus, as I became lost in her, infatuated by her. I lowered my head and began placing gentle kisses on her beautiful tan thighs and knees. I felt her fingers softly running through my hair. I lifted her left foot and slid off her sandal, then did the same with the right one. I got up on the bed and began kissing her as we slowly descended onto the soft blanket covering the bed. I reached up to grab a pillow and pull it down as she lifted her head and smiled, I tucked it under, and she laid her head on it. I remember the five-year difference in our ages playing tricks on my mind and not wanting to rush anything. Our hands wandered and explored each other's bodies as we continued to passionately kiss. Then she began to slowly unbutton her shirt, our eyes locked, and without a word she assured me she was comfortable. In a gentle way I separated her shirt to reveal a beautiful black lace bra that accented her perfectly tanned skin. I could feel my breathing intensify as my testosterone levels radiated throughout my body. My controlled demeanor was now lost to mutually unconstrained sexual desires.

Even now as I recollect that evening, I can feel my heart beating faster. My body has never forgotten.

"After a drink or two and a few slow dances at the piano bar, we left and walked to the far end of the ship and found an unoccupied lounge chair. We only needed one as we now had this sharing thing down to a science. Keri leaned back into me and I wrapped my arms around her to keep her warm from the cool air of the early morning. We overheard another couple saying they could faintly see the lights shining from the port of Miami, where we would soon dock.

We got up and I moved the chair closer to the railing so we could have a view of the lights and port as well.

It was magical yet sad."

"Sad because it was your last night together?"

"Yes. And because I was not sure I would ever see Keri again.

The darkness was now fading, and the port was becoming clearer. The speed of the ship had slowed down. Keri's watch told us it was almost 6am and she knew she had to get back to her cabin in case her parents checked on the two girls. Neither of us wanted to leave, we were so comfortable lying together, wishing this night did not have to end.

Everybody else around us was gone. I walked Keri to her cabin and kissed her goodnight. We planned to meet in a few hours and say goodbye. She hugged me so tight and I remember her eyes filling with tears. It was amazing the impact just several days and nights together had on us. The magic and mystery of the ocean, the grace and beauty of the islands, the luxuriousness of that magnificent ship. All those factors played a part.

I had that same empty feeling I experienced each of the nights I left her and walked alone back to my cabin. The guys were sound asleep. I changed into shorts and T-shirt and passed out. I did not have to worry about setting an alarm, Bill took care of that as he did every morning.

Sure enough, it seemed like just minutes later, Bill was letting us know we had to wake up. Luckily, we packed the night before.

As we got dressed, we could hear a lot of movement outside. It was going to be chaotic as thousands of passengers were heading for the exits with luggage in hand.

So many buses and shuttles were waiting to take people to airports or parking garages. Since Keri's cabin was so much further from mine, I wondered if I would see her. As we maneuvered through the narrow decks of the ship, I could only focus on looking above heads trying to find her.

We finally got off the ship and huddled near a pillar of the underground parking area. Bill went off to try and locate our hotel shuttle, since we had reservations to stay in Miami several days before flying back home, the hotel was providing us with free shuttle transportation. Tony and I scanned the area. Suddenly from the corner of my eye I could see someone approaching me, I turned quickly, and it was Keri. Her smile and bedroom eyes immediately put me at ease. I let go of my suitcase handle and took her in my arms.

We had already exchanged addresses and phone numbers."

"This was back in the old days Angelina, before email was a thing, or skype was created, and no social media." With my arm around her I shook her a bit as she laughed.

"And now the hard part came when we would have to part ways and say goodbye, not sure if or when we would ever see each other again.

From a distance we could see her mom waving for her to come join them. I did not really want to be around her and Tonia's parents, but I sensed they needed to leave, and Bill hadn't returned yet, so I walked her over.

As we approached, Keri's mother said their shuttle was there to take them to the airport. They would fly out and she would be home in a few hours while I had a few more days and nights there in Miami. I told the four parents and the little brother that it was nice meeting them, then gave Tonia a hug, and Keri one last hug and kiss. As we slowly peeled our bodies apart, I reached for her hands, they were perfect, soft as silk and so tanned, I just loved holding them. We looked into each other's eyes and said good-bye. I still remember that sad empty feeling. How could I feel so deeply for a girl I had only known for four days? Yet I did.

She suddenly embraced me again and gave me one last kiss. Her eyes were tear filled and that added to my sadness. I already knew I would have to call her that evening, to hear her voice again, feel that amazing connection, if even just through the phone.

As I watched her walk away, I could hear Tony telling me Bill was coming back, yet it seemed like he was 100 miles away. Nothing mattered more to me at that moment then to watch Keri walk through the crowd and smiling every time she turned to give me another last wave, until that final one when she finally boarded the shuttle and it drove off and eventually out of sight."

No other woman has ever had such an effect on me. It was intense, magical, exciting, yet felt like my 23 yr. old heart was breaking for the first time. I could not understand it. We had only spent four days together.

"Let's get you to bed my little Angel, we have a long day ahead of us and we need to wake up early and catch the boat."

"But grandpa I want to hear about Miami and you calling Keri."

I could see she was intrigued and honestly, it feels good talking about it after all these years.

"Ok listen, I will finish the story up when we are in Sirmione." I said, while getting up and walking her to her room.

As we got to the door of her room she stopped and looked up at me.

"Grandpa, do you miss Keri?"

Hearing my granddaughter ask me that brought it to a reality for me. Surprisingly without hesitation I responded.

"I do."

I kissed her on the forehead as always and said goodnight.

I went to pour myself another glass of wine, then went out and sat on the deck. I stared at the beautiful dark sky that was glistening from the luminous light of the stars. I wondered where Keri might be, and what she is doing at this exact moment. If she ever thinks of me, the way I am thinking of her now.

I found myself imagining her next to me just like we were that last night of the cruise as we drifted into the Miami harbor so many years ago. I have imagined this very scenario thousands of times over the years. A beautiful song by my favorite Italian opera singer Andrea Bocelli called, *Mille Lune, Mille Onde,* (1000 moons, 1000 waves) comes to mind every time. I scrolled through the playlist on my phone, until I found it. I adjusted the volume and hit play, as Andrea sang this beautiful song in Italian.

A thousand Moons a thousand waves
Wake up my love
The nights already over
Wake up come here in my arms
The sun is rising
Don't think of the past
All the mist that lies there
Hug me talk to me again
And you'll see we'll live again
Bind my heart with your hair
You're my wave breaking inside me
Hug me for now I'm the sea
You'll feel the thrill right through
Talk to me.
Hold me
Glide
Blue moon
Leaves and the wind carries us
We're heading skywards
Hug me and let yourself go
Now you are the wind
Bind my heart with your hair
You're my wave breaking inside me
Hug me for now I'm the sea
You'll feel the thrill right through
And the night's slip by
I glide kissing you
A thousand moons a thousand waves
That cross our sea
Bind my heart with your hair
You'll feel the thrill right through.

I finished my wine and went to bed.

Chapter 16

Morning came quickly and I was excited for our trip, maybe not quite as excited as Angelina was as I already heard her moving about the house.

I showered and dressed before emerging from my room to find her dressed, her suitcase by the door, and wearing her backpack, just sitting waiting for me.

"Good morning grandpa, I'm so glad you finally woke up." She said smirking.

"OK OK I'm ready, let's go. We can get something to eat before boarding the boat."

We squeezed our two suitcases and a few other things into the tiny back seat of my convertible and drove off to town.

We parked at the docks and I secured the top and doors as we walked to the boat.

It was a beautiful boat that conducted tours up and down the lake that maybe had a capacity of 100 people. A crew member greeted us and checked us in while another member tagged our luggage and took it away to store it.

We would be sailing for roughly 2 hrs. before reaching our destination. The drive is beautiful as well but travelling down the lake is something I don't do often and its simply spectacular and would be a first for Angelina.

There were no assigned seats, you could sit inside or outside on the deck. Tables and chairs were spread out all over to give guests personal space while taking in the views from every angle.

I was hungry and in need of coffee so I suggested we go into the café and order up some breakfast.

Angelina went and found us a table for two facing the water as I ordered at the counter. She just wanted cereal and orange juice as I got eggs toast and home fries.

I carried our drinks over and sat down. We looked out and just enjoyed the view while sipping from our cups waiting for our food.

We could feel the boat pushing away from the dock and slowly making its way towards the center of the lake before accelerating to a comfortable cruising speed.

Our food arrived and we made small talk as we ate. Afterwards we went out to the deck and found a few chairs together. The boat appeared to be at maybe 50% capacity which made it nice.

Angelina held onto the railing just feet away from me as she absorbed the amazing views while we traveled down the lake. I was checking email and corresponding through texts with David about meeting for dinner this evening.

"Angel, are you OK with a friend of mine meeting us for dinner tonight?"

"Sure grandpa. Does he live in Italy?

"No, he is an old friend from work. He lives in the states but is here on business so we thought we would catch up over dinner."

"Just him?"

"Yep, just him."

The crew had announced that we were just twenty minutes from our destination so Angelina and I began walking towards the area where we would exit.

Seemed like about half the passengers were departing here as well, with the remaining staying aboard for the round-trip package.

The docks here were a little more glamourous than the ones back home to appeal more towards the tourist staying at these amazing resorts.

I had planned for a hotel shuttle to be waiting for us. We docked and exited quite quickly as I handed the crew member my luggage tags and he quickly unloaded our two suitcases. I tipped him and thanked him. I had already spotted the hotel van. As we walked over to it the driver addressed us.

"Mr. DeMarco?"

"Yes."

"Welcome sir. And hello little signorina."

"Hello." Angelina responded as she waved to him.

He put our luggage into the rear of the van as we climbed into the back seat. It was a short drive that we could have easily walked but with the warm humid air, two suitcases, a carrying case for me and backpack for Angelina, the ride was most convenient.

We drove by a strip of stores and saw the large market area off in the distance as Angelina gasped.

"Grandpa!"

"Yes, we are coming down later or tomorrow OK."

"Can't wait, looks so awesome."

I smiled and gave her a one arm hug.

Soon, the spectacular spa complex came into view. It has been at least a year since I have visited here and just seeing it gave me an invigorating sensation. It's beautiful historic buildings, landscaping, statues and fountains make it such a lavishing oasis.

"OMG grandpa."

She already had her phone out taking pictures as we drove past the security guards and into this enormous complex.

We pulled up into the circular drive of our hotel. The driver quickly got out and opened the door for us then he took out our luggage as a hotel bellman greeted us and transferred our bags onto a cart.

I tipped the driver generously because I knew we would need rides to and from the town strip, and drivers are usually a little more attentive to guests they know tip well.

"Cool uniforms." Angelina whispered to me, referencing to the bellman.

"They sure are." I responded with a smirk.

The uniforms resembled something from the Romanesque days.

We checked in and made our way to the elevator. I reserved a suite on the third floor.

The elevators are somewhat smaller than ones in the states. I told the bellman I had it from here and tipped him, knowing full well the small elevator would be cramped with another adult in there and assured him the cart would be outside my suite for him to pick up later. There are only three floors, with twenty rooms per floor, so having two elevators minimizes the wait time.

The suite was top notch. We each had our own bedroom equipped with a full bathroom, king size bed, walk in closet, television, and mini refrigerator.

Angelina felt like she was in heaven.

The Wi-Fi connection was a little slow, but she finally connected to facetime with her mom. I could hear her voice raising as she described her room and the hotel. She must have said she loves Italy twenty times before making her way into my room carrying her laptop with my daughter in laws smiling face on the screen.

I stopped unpacking.

"Hello Marla!"

"Hello Dad! I see you are truly spoiling my little girl."

"Me?"

We both began laughing with Angelina joining in.

"What's this place called again grandpa?"

"The Virgillo & Catullo spa complex. It is in Sirmione, less than two hours from my home. Thought we would take a little escape."

Marla was just smiling shaking her head.

"I want that little escape." She blurted out.

"Anytime!" I replied.

"And mom, we took a boat here. We sailed from the dock in grandpa's town right to the dock here."

"Sounds absolutely amazing. How long are you staying?"

"Just two nights. And we just happen to have appointments at the spa in a little while."

"Oh, now you really are spoiling her."

Angelina's eyes lit up and her jaw dropped.

"Yep, were going to get facials. I'm hoping it makes me look younger."

Marla and Angelina burst out laughing.

"Really grandpa, were really going to the spa and getting a facial."

"Yes, we are."

"Well, I will let you and grandpa get ready for your spa treatments. You two enjoy, and facetime me later OK Angelina, when dad will be here so we can both chat with you and grandpa."

"Sounds good mom I love you."

"Love you too sweetheart. Love you to dad, thank you for everything."

"Love you and it's my pleasure spoiling her."

"I see that."

"Bye mom!"

"Bye!"

They each signed off and I told Angelina to put on her swimsuit and that there should be a big fluffy robe in the bathroom closet for her to wear.

She tucked her laptop under her arm and trotted off.

Marla's father passed away in a car accident years ago, when her and my son had just started dating. In my own way, I looked after her as if she were my own daughter. She eased into calling me Dad on occasion, then it became very natural, and I was completely okay with it.

I finished unpacking and changed into my shorts and robe then I met Angelina in the large living room that separated our bedrooms.

"You look absolutely adorable."

"Thank you." She replied, while spinning in a circle for me like some runway model.

The robe was a little too big for her but made her look even more cute as it was almost dragging.

"Grandpa did you see this?"

She pointed to a large basket of various fresh fruits, a covered cheese platter with a variety of crackers, and many different bottles of juice and soda on ice, all displayed on a table.

I walked over and opened the envelope resting against the basket.

"Who is it from grandpa?"

"The hotel manager. He's become a friend over the last five years and a very good customer."

"Oh, he buy's wine from you?"

"Yes. This was a good faith gesture, awfully nice of him."

"That was so nice of him grandpa, we can just eat all this and not even go to the restaurant." She said laughing, popping a grape into her mouth.

"Come on kiddo lets go." I said, laughing back.

We still had almost an hour before our appointments, so we walked the halls, and I showed her around.

Almost everyone was wearing the same beautiful robes because the main attraction here was the award-winning magnificent spas.

We reached the spa and entered through the large glass doors adorned by large Romanesque pillars. Everything was made from marble and perfectly sculptured stonework. The music and pleasant scent immediately relaxed your entire body.

We made our way to the desk while taking in the beauty. We were then escorted into an area with many small private mineral baths meant for no more than two people. We were served a drink of our choice as we took off our robes and laid them on a small rack. The water was warm and soothing, we each sunk into a molded seat.

We were told our therapists would come for us in fifteen minutes and they ran on strict schedules to accommodate their busy schedules each day yet kept the most relaxing and pleasant demeanor. I made it clear when I placed the reservation that we would have facials in the same room.

We did not speak much, just leaned back and enjoyed the warm water and tiny soothing bubbles firing from the many jets lining the walls of the tub, as we sipped on our refreshing iced tea.

Soon the therapists arrived. Two young ladies that almost looked like sisters, but we later found out they were of no relation.

They handed each of us a towel and we patted ourselves dry, put our robes back on, and followed them to a private dimly lit room with two reclining chairs draped with excellent quality sheets and blanket.

Angelina was in heaven. She was genuinely enjoying every second of this pampering experience.

An hour seemed to fly by, but it was amazing. It is not too often I pamper myself and I was lost in the tranquility.

At the end, the therapists told each of us to relax for a few minutes then come out when we were ready.

"Grandpa that was AMAZING." She emphasized.

"I totally agree. I could lay here forever."

"Me to."

After about ten minutes I suggested we get up and walk out. One of the therapists was outside the door and showed us back to the mineral spa, where we spent about another twenty minutes and had another drink. This time I chose wine.

After, Angelina wanted to go through another set of doors which led to an amazing inground pool made from stone formations. I appreciate the craftmanship and attention to every detail of this entire place, its spectacular. But to a twelve-year-old, it is more like an indoor/outdoor waterpark with some perks.

Angelina wasted no time jumping into the pool. I walked down the stairs and joined her in the water.

I loved watching my granddaughter having such a good time.

A waitress came over and asked if we wanted anything. I ordered another glass of wine and Angelina wanted a lemonade. I also ordered some snacks.

We took a brief break from swimming to enjoy the snacks and drinks. Angelina especially enjoyed the thin cheese sticks and crusty slices of bread as I ate the thinly sliced meats, bread, and cheese.

After about an hour we agreed to leave and take a long walk around the complex before heading up to our suite.

Angelina found it so amusing to walk around the entire place wearing robes.

"We are having dinner in two hours Angel. If you get hungry, have something from this basket."

"OK grandpa. I had enough at the pool. I'm just going to relax in my bedroom and go on my laptop."

"Don't forget, my friend David will be meeting us."

"I know."

Chapter 17

As Angelina disappeared into her bedroom, I went into mine to shower, shave, and just watch some TV until I needed to get dressed.

I would later discover that Angelina had found the letters that I had received from Keri all those years ago. They were in a separate envelope inside the same box the postcards were in and the photos from the cruise with Keri.

Angelina later confessed that she did not read the letters but simply wrote down Keri's first and last name as well as her address.

While she was alone in her bedroom, she began searching for Keri's name on the popular social media sites.

Apparently, she was not having much luck. But was able to find several women with hyphenated names which included Keri's maiden name.

In a risky and bold move Angelina sent messages to six women. One responded almost immediately and said she is not the woman Angelina was searching for.

She must have been planning this for days since I began telling her the story of Keri. Hearing her tell her mom how she felt I must be lonely. It all added up, and now she wanted to make a connection to see if she could contact Keri and possibly play matchmaker.

Angelina nervously waited for replies as she searched other social media sites but being a teen, she knew which site was used mostly by the older population.

She has spent enough time with me over the years to have developed certain spy qualities aside from being a very smart girl.

She has seen photos of Keri and knew which state she lived in years ago, so I am sure her messages were to women resembling those attributes.

Chapter 18

The time passed quickly, and I was suddenly taken out of my semi-conscious state by the sound of an incoming text message from David. He was letting me know he had arrived and was having a drink at the bar. I responded back letting him know we would be down shortly.

Thinking back, Angelina seemed a little taken off guard when I yelled for her from my room that it was time to get ready. Her response seemed a bit suspicious, like she was unexpectedly caught doing something she should not have been doing.

"OK grandpa, I'll be ready in five minutes."

The restaurants here were very casual, most men wore a sport jacket without ties. That would be my attire for the evening. Even in warmer temperatures I often wore a sport jacket because I enjoyed the luxury of having pockets inside the coat rather than having bulky necessities protruding from the pockets of my pants.

We met in the living room and Angelina looked simply beautiful.

She was wearing a cute little sundress and had fixed her hair into a lovely ponytail, and wore two rings and a bracelet, along with a little handbag.

"You look absolutely beautiful my little Angel."

"Thanks Grandpa!"

We made our way to the elevator. From the first floor we maneuvered through several hallways to the restaurant I chose that evening. I could see David as we entered and were greeted by a hostess. I told her my name as she checked her tablet and grabbed three menus. I asked her to give me a minute as I walked over and greeted my old friend. We shook hands and were both happy to see each other.

I introduced him to Angelina.

"Nice to meet you David, Angelina said extending her hand."

David shook her hand as he looked at me.

"Is she the most adorable and delightful girl ever?"

"Yes, she is." I replied laughing

"So nice to finally meet you. Your grandfather has told me so much about you over the years."

To most, I am very closed and introverted. There are very few select people close enough to me in which I offer information to, especially regarding my family. David had my trust, so he was one of those people.

I nodded to the hostess and she led the way to our booth tucked away in a corner, just as I requested with my reservation.

David and I spoke casually during this short walk.

He was carrying a thin black briefcase; one I recognized all too well. He took a taxi from the train and would then return to Rome after dinner. This is what life was like for an intelligence officer.

I normally prefer Angelina not use technology devices during dinner, but this evening would be an exception so she was not bored, and her attention diverted elsewhere and not on the classified documents I would be looking at during this dinner meeting.

David had laid the briefcase upside down with his hand resting on top. This was no ordinary briefcase made for civilians. It was a modified version that intelligence agencies use. If someone were to open this briefcase right side up and pressing both buttons simultaneously it would explode, destroying the contents of the case and the person opening it. This would assure classified material would not fall into the wrong hands.

I have never been one to delay matters, so I got right to the point.

"So, what are we looking at David?"

Knowing my personality, he then opened the briefcase, as it was designed to be correctly opened, and took out a rather thin large envelope marked CLASSIFIED.

I immediately flipped it over and kept it flat on the table, opening it and sliding out the contents.

Angelina did not seem phased or even interested in our conversation.

"Are you chatting with girlfriends?"

"Yep."

Little did I know she was monitoring one of her social media accounts hoping to hear from one of the Keri's she messaged.

I could see a young female waitress walking briskly towards our table.

"Good evening!" She said with a big smile.

We almost all replied in unison.

"Good evening."

"Would you like to start off with a drink as you take your time looking over the menu?"

"Sure."

As soon as we finished ordering drinks our waitress informed us of several specials on the menu this evening as well as a few unique new appetizers.

In a world-renowned resort like this, the wait staff are usually bilingual and almost everyone speaks English well. The hostess knew from our brief interaction that we spoke English, so she gave us menus translated in English.

"I know what I'm getting." Angelina blurted out.

"Let me guess, your favorite?"

"Yep." She answered with a smile.

"What's your favorite?" David asked.

"Ravioli."

After a minute or so David and I each laid down our menu. I then lifted the thin stack of papers and breezed through them to get the jest of what David may have been interested in. I knew the waitress would be back very shortly and did not want any eyes catching even a glimpse of these papers.

"Here you go. And here are some fresh rolls. By the way, my name is Ciara."

"Hello Ciara!" Angelina remarked with a small wave of her hand.

"Hello." Ciara smiled back at Angelina.

"Have you had the chance to look over the menu?"

"Yes." I replied. "And I think we are all ready to order. Angelina would you like to go first."

"Sure, I will have the ravioli."

"The petite portion of two, or four? They are kind of large ravioli."

"Just two."

I glanced at David.

"I will have the sautéed chicken with vegetables and pasta."

"And I will have the Delmonico steak, medium well, with brown rice. And can we also have an order of tomato and basil bruschetta for an appetizer."

"Absolutely, anything else?"

"No thank you." David responded.

As she walked away, I began looking at the documents again, and noticed several photos.

"Do you recognize these two?"

"Yes."

"What can you tell me about them?"

"They were both radical terrorists. One was from Kenya, the other from Pakistan."

As I pointed to each photo.

"They became acquainted while they were each attending Arizona State University in Tempe Arizona. They associated with several mosques throughout Arizona to recruit like-minded radicals. They eventually devised a plot to detonate several bombs simultaneously throughout LA, including LAX."

"We extinguished him." I said under my breath, and pointing to one of the photos, as to not draw any attention from Angelina.

"And the other one is serving life in a British prison."

"Not anymore."

"What?"

"Somehow British officials made a deal to release him back to Kenya to finish out his sentence, but something went astray, and he never made it to Kenya, according to officials."

"And these documents." I asked.

Just then I could see Ciara coming our way.

"There you are." She said, while placing the plate of appetizers and a large bowl of salad in the middle of the table."

"Thank you." I commented. Then she walked away.

"They have the best salad dressing." I remarked as Angelina put a little pile of salad on her plate and took a piece of bruschetta.

I noticed Angelina's smile turn to a frown as she stared at her phone.

"What's wrong?"

"Me?" She asked.

"Yes."

"Oh nothing. Just reading a message."

I would later find out two more Keri's responded that they were not who she was looking for. That was three out of the six.

I looked back at David.

"These documents are communications we've intercepted and also classified documentation from CSIS."

Which is the Canadian Security Intelligence Service.

"Canada believes this guy is now there and has been recruiting radicals from several mosques in close proximity of the US border and planning an attack on the US from Canada."

"He is obviously living under a new identity."

"Yes. But we think he is also living in one of these mosques since he is well funded and could easily make bribes. I know you have Muslim connections throughout the world. Can you tap your resources and help me with this?"

"You want me to find out where he is living."

"I need your help Anthony. They put me in charge of this and I can't blow it."

I began eating my salad rather quickly, also managing to enjoy two bruschetta's while glancing through the papers, reading parts that seemed important to me.

David made small talk with Angelina, asking her how she liked Italy, if she missed home, and if I was spoiling her like a grandfather should.

I could hear her telling him all about the spa, and her facial, the cool bathrobe and disposable slippers she loved so much that she is keeping them.

Ciara now returned with our meals along with a young man who would clear away the salad bowl and plates to make room for Ciara to lay down our entrees.

"Would you like another bottle of wine?"

"Yes please." I answered.

"And another lemonade?"

"Yes please." Angelina replied.

The lemonade in Italy was not like minute maid lemonade in the states. Here it is made from fresh home-grown lemons, with just the right amount of sugar to make it perfect.

"The food looks absolutely amazing." David commented.

Angelina and I both agreed.

As we began to eat Ciara returned with another bottle of wine, she uncorked it and offered us to taste it once again."

"Not necessary Ciara, we know this is the best."

"It sure is one of our most popular wines," she replied. Totally unaware I owned the winery from which it is made.

"Anthony I'm sorry, we got so engulfed with work, that I hadn't even thought to look at the label and notice this is yours."

"It's OK. But you must like it, you already had two glasses and about to have a few more."

"I love it." He responded. "It's amazing actually."

"Thank you."

I could see Angelina smiling at us as she was separating her raviolis into tiny bite size pieces using her fork.

I ate my rice first while finishing up with the papers then slid them back into the envelope.

"I will be back home in two days and will look into this then."

"Thank you, Anthony, greatly appreciated."

David understood I would need the secure connections from my home to make such inquiries and not public Wi-Fi in this hotel. Even with a VPN I still did not trust anything public.

I could see a sign of relief on David's face.

Many times, terrorists will seek refuge in religious establishments because for the most part they are safe havens, and almost always the leaders are not willingly condoning it, they are usually threatened with death if they disagree with the terrorists and many religious leaders have been murdered as a result.

The connections and alliances I have developed over thirty years are priceless in the intel world. And even now, "retired" from the agency, I am being asked once again to activate these resources for my country and my friend, it must be done. My oath remains honored.

The business part was over and now I could enjoy my steak and wine.

We caught up on old times but tried to keep Angelina in the loop as best we could.

She, of course, was preoccupied with her phone, and monitoring the little scheme she had going on.

"I'm still grateful for the time you brought me along as part of your team to advise President Bush."

"Grandpa you met a president?"

"Over the years I've met several presidents. Some I liked, others I did not. I was acting on behalf of my agency as an advisor, to brief the president on more than likely a critical matter involving national security."

"That's so cool."

I smiled at her and sort of rolled my eyes.

David then looked at Angelina.

"But the time I'm talking about, was a meeting at the president's private ranch in Texas while he was on vacation."

"That was pretty cool and the first time I was ever at an actual ranch. Crawford Texas, I will never forget." I added.

The briefing David spoke of was about eight weeks prior to the 9/11 attacks on the US. Our agency had been collaborating with intelligence agencies in Belgium, Cyprus, France, Germany, Italy, Japan, Monte Carlo, the Netherlands, and Switzerland, over growing concerns of suspicious trading in the world stock markets. We had incredible evidence that insider trading was going on at a grand scale level involving the airline industries, financial and reinsurance companies, as well as other financial vehicles.

The briefing was effective and the president, being a very down to earth man, took this information very seriously. I was point blank honest with him and informed him that all of this had signs of something big going down and would be very profitable to the people behind this activity.

His administration failed to authorize further investigations. The director of my agency was sent a memo from the White House stating that the people and organizations we named as being a part of this suspicious activity were viewed as, "unlikely," to have been associated with our suggested perpetrators, such as the terrorist group al Qaeda.

And eight weeks later 9/11 happened, and many people stood to make a fortune off the misfortune that wreaked havoc on the United States.

I could see in the distance the manager making his way towards us as he greeted other guests enjoying dinner along the way.

As he approached, I stood up.

"Mario, how are you?"

"Excellent Anthony, how are you?"

"Great! Just enjoying a few days here with my granddaughter Angelina."

"Hello." Angelina said with a smile.

"What a beautiful young lady and with a beautiful name. My sisters name is Angelina."

David stood up during Mario's interaction with my granddaughter.

Mario paused so I could introduce them.

"And this is David, an old colleague visiting from the states."

"Welcome Signore. You are on vacation?"

"Not really, I have business in Rome, and had to visit my old friend."

"I hope you all are enjoying your meals?"

"Yes." We all replied in unison.

Mario slid the bottle of wine from the ice bucket just enough to read the label.

"But of course." He commented with a smile.

"Of course." I replied.

Mario then looked around quickly until he spotted Ciara and motioned for her to come over.

She must have thought she was in trouble or did something wrong.

"Ciara, bring my friends a sample platter of every dessert we have. Desserts and coffee are on me."

"Mario, that's not…"

"You are my friend and one of my most faithful suppliers. It's my pleasure to offer this."

We all thanked him.

"Ciara, do you know who this man is?"

"No."

Mario lifted the bottle of wine from the bucket again.

"This gentleman produces this wine."

Her puzzled look now formed a big smile.

"Why didn't you tell me signore. I love this wine."

I just smiled back.

"I will go get the dessert platter ready. Would anyone like coffee, tea, or an expresso?"

"Coffee for me."

"I will have an expresso." David replied, I still have a long train ride back to Rome.

"I'm good." Angelina said.

Dessert came and everything was delicious. Of course, we could not finish the dozen or so items on the platter, so we had it wrapped.

Ciara returned to ask if we needed anything else. After almost two hours of eating, drinking, taking care of business, and catching up with David, we were ready to leave, and I knew Angelina had to be bored by now although she refused to show any signs of it.

"I think we are all set."

"Should I just apply the bill to your room signore?"

"No." David blurted.

"I got this." As he reached for the check.

"David, you are my guest, let me get this."

"No, I insist." He said handing Ciara his gold American Express card.

When Ciara returned, David signed, and Angelina and I walked with him to the lobby.

The life of a covert officer does not leave much room for pleasurable vacations or time off. You are always on duty and always on guard.

"Give me a second." David said as he walked to the concierge desk. No doubt to have them summon a taxi or provide a shuttle for him to the train station.

The information we discussed was already committed to memory and the envelope concealing the classified documents was secured in his briefcase.

"I will look into that as soon as I return home and get back to you."

"Thank you." David replied as he extended his right arm to shake my hand. "once again I owe you a debt of gratitude."

I smirked and nodded my head in agreement.

"Angelina, it was a pleasure meeting you and I hope to see you again someday."

"Nice meeting you as well David."

I could see David's relaxed facial expressions then turn to something more like a sense of urgency. I remember those days. You were only in the moment for that moment, but your mind was many steps ahead. He glanced at the concierge who gave David a nod and a signal that a car was waiting.

I grabbed David's shoulder with a firm grip and looked him directly in the eye.

"Be careful. I will be in touch."

For a moment, his face released its tension.

"Thank you, my friend."

And with that he briskly walked and followed the concierge through the doors.

When an officer goes from being overt to covert their entire life changes. They usually are paired with a mentor and that mentor is responsible for teaching the mentee how to survive in this new covert lifestyle, while still being a fully productive officer. I was David's mentor. Over the years I have had many mentees. Not all are cut out for this job. Actually, most are not. Many do not even last a few years. I always feel a sense of responsibility for the people I have mentored. I lost one once. It was no fault of my own, but I am reminded of it every day.

Chapter 19

The evening was still young, and I knew Angelina would love to go down to the markets. It is even more beautiful at night because everything is lit up with live music playing.

"What do you say we go down to the markets and maybe shop a little?"

"Yes!" She responded without hesitation.

"Ok, let's see if we can get a ride down."

The concierge had a shuttle available, and we left immediately.

Tipping the hotel staff always goes a long way so I make sure I have plenty of euros on hand.

We got into the back seat of the shuttle.

"Did you enjoy dinner and dessert."

"It was so good, and I am so full."

We both laughed.

"I am too." I replied.

"I'm sorry David and I talked so much but we haven't seen each other in a few years, and he had some work stuff to run by me."

"It's OK grandpa, but I thought you were retired from the agency."

"Well, technically I am. But, I still do some consulting, when the need arises."

"I get it."

"You looked pretty busy on your phone throughout dinner."

"Yeah, I was just checking posts from my friends and stuff."

"Anything interesting going on with the girls."

"Not really, you know, just girl stuff."

I burst out laughing.

"That's exactly what your aunt Emery use to say to me."

At that point four of the Keri's had responded with no luck. I am sure Angelina's hopes were becoming bleak.

We arrived and the driver pulled over to the curb. Cars were not allowed in the market area. I gave the driver a generous tip and asked if he could pick us back up in this exact spot in one hour. He agreed and thanked me.

We then walked about thirty feet and entered the market area. The road was paved with cobble stones, so you had to be careful of your footing. The smell of various foods and desserts lingered in the air just tempting you to try something, that reminded me of a carnival. Of course, we were full, and I was still carrying a bag filled with desserts left over from dinner.

My intention was to walk around, enjoy the atmosphere, and maybe let Angelina shop for a few things. The entire market area was roughly one large city block. Most shoppers were tourists and undoubtably staying in one of the several beautiful upscale hotels, enjoying the spas during the day and roaming the market area by night. All seemed relaxed and in pleasant moods. We could hear different languages and accents fading in and out while walking as several live musical acts were strategically placed throughout the market so one did not overwhelm the other.

We strolled along, peeking into the many different enclosures as well as viewing the variety of open carts and stands, each selling their own unique items. The enclosed shops were basically just nice tents that offered more valuable clothing, shoes, jewelry, and a few even selling electronic devices, and usually had one plain clothes security officer lurking around just to make sure nothing was robbed since there were no security cameras, alarms, or walk-through detectors. At the end of the night the merchants would load up their goods and drive off, only leaving an empty tent or stand behind until the next afternoon.

Angelina stayed close to me because some merchants could be a bit aggressive trying to intrigue you to buy from them. I do not come across as a tourist so most just greeted us or nodded.

"Let me know if you see anything you like. I was thinking maybe we could find you a dress or something for dinner tomorrow night."

Angelina was a real girlie girl. She loved cute dresses, painting her nails, purses, lip gloss, trying different styles with her hair, and so on, so I knew she would love picking out a dress. She reminded me so much of my daughter Emery at that age.

I could see a clothing store on the other side of the street, so we made our way to it.

Two young women seemed to be running it and currently busy with customers, so we began glancing at the different racks.

This market area was well known, and the vendors only carried excellent quality products. They were aware of how expensive these hotels and spas were and knew people came here to enjoy themselves and spend money, but not on junk or poor-quality items.

Angelina quickly found several racks that had sizes in her range, obviously my daughter in law has helped equip her with such skill.

I was enjoying the expressions on my granddaughter's face as she flipped through the circular racks. She had pulled off several dresses and laid them on top of the rack before one of the young ladies made her way over to us.

"Buonasera. Mi chiamo Maria. Desidera?" (*Good Evening, my name is Maria. May I help you?*)

"Hello Maria! Yes, my granddaughter is looking for a dress."

"I speak English also." Maria said, with a smile.

"Hello there!"

"Hello." Angelina responded in a shy why.

"Are you interested in one of these?" Maria asked, pointing to the dresses Angelina had laid out.

"Yes."

"Would you like to try them on and see which one you might like?"

"Sure."

Maria smiled and looked over at me. She could sense Angelina's shyness.

"Follow me over to the changing room."

After trying on three dresses Angelina decided on an aqua blue sundress that looked amazing against her tan skin, brown hair, and beautiful blue eyes.

I was not surprised to find it a bit pricey, but it was well worth it.

"Thank you so much grandpa."

"You are so welcome Angel." I replied bending down to hug her.

Maria smiled at us, appreciating the affection I shared with my granddaughter, and then continued checking us out. I glanced at my watch and realized we only had twenty minutes left before the driver would be meeting us.

I told Angelina we would come back and visit again tomorrow during the day when the street would most likely be a little less crowded and we could have lunch here.

As we strolled back to our meeting point, I noticed a cart with all kinds of jewelry.

"What do you say we find you a cute bracelet to match that new dress?"

"Are you sure grandpa?"

"Of course, I'm sure."

A woman who I would say was in her mid to late thirties was sitting in a chair next to the cart and greeted us.

I am sure she is used to many potential customers just glancing and then moving on.

"Let me know if you see anything you like signorina."

"I will."

Most people were joyful and happy walking around, engaging in conversation, plastic glasses of wine or beer in hand sold by market vendors.

"Do you like this grandpa?"

It was a bracelet made of tiny blue topaz-colored stones, almost the exact color of her dress.

"I love it, it matches your dress perfectly."

"You found something?" The woman asked rising from her chair.

"Yes, we will take this."

"Would you like to wear it now signorina?" She asked opening the clasp and gesturing to attach it around Angelina's wrist."

Angelina looked up at me and I nodded in an assuring way.

"Sure." Angelina responded holding out her right closed fist.

The woman quickly attached it and then cashed me out.

"Grazie!" She said handing me my change.

"Have a good evening." I replied as we began walking.

Looking ahead I could see the driver standing outside of the shuttle leaning on the hood taking in the sights as he waited for us.

As he saw us approach, he opened the back door and I climbed in behind Angelina as she scooted over to the other side.

I thanked the driver for keeping his word as he gently pulled from the curd and headed in the direction of our hotel.

Angelina gazed out of the window admiring the lights and how everything looked so much different at night.

We passed several decorative fountains as we drove past a few hotels before reaching our own. Angelina especially loved the several-colored lights shining on the fountains and reflecting off the water giving it a mystical appearance.

By the time we reached the hotel and made our way to the room we were both a bit tired.

Before entering the room, I glanced at the rug then at the door jam. I could see the tiny corner of a folded piece of paper I had placed there before we left. It was an old habit of mine as a security measure to detect if anyone had entered the room while I was gone. Place the "Do Not Disturb" sign on the door and the piece of paper in the door jam. If housekeeping truly obeyed the sign, the paper should still be in the exact position you left it. If not, get hotel security.

Angelina liked using the electronic entry card, so I let her unlock and open the door as I reached out my hand and caught the falling folded piece of paper.

"I had such a great time today grandpa." Angelina said as she gave me a hug.

"I cannot wait to wear my new dress tomorrow."

"I am so glad you had fun."

"Grandpa let's put on our pajamas and then you can finish telling me about Miami and you calling Keri."

"You're not letting this story go, are you?"

"Nope." She said with her big smile. "It's way to interesting grandpa."

"OK let's get changed and meet in the living room area on that comfy looking sofa."

I came out of my bedroom first and walked over to the basket of fruits and stuff. I put some crackers on a napkin and then opened the mini fridge and took out a one serving size bottle of wine and went over to get comfortable.

Angelina was checking her social media account again and I am sure disappointed to see that she had still not received responses from two of the women.

In her world, young people communicated with social media in real time, instant responses. But, for the more mature crowd, social media is not such a priority, it is more of a novelty, for many of us at least.

Within a few minutes Angelina emerged from her room.

"Have some fruit or something, and there are drinks and the rest of the desserts in the fridge."

She grabbed a bunch of grapes and came over and plopped next to me. She covered herself up with an incredibly soft blanket and then leaned into me.

"So, the cruise ended, you and Keri said goodbye, she was flying back home, and you were staying in Miami."

"Yes. It was such a sad moment as we went our separate ways. Thousands of passengers all frantically trying to locate taxis and shuttles to bring them wherever they needed to be. I hated leaving her in that chaos because all our time was in a very relaxed low-key environment that we created, but here, it was chaos. We could not control it.

So, me and the guys put our suitcases into the rear of the shuttle van and the driver quickly drove off. The heat was unbearable for guys growing up on the east coast.

We asked the driver to slow down so we could enjoy the views of downtown Miami."

"Is it nice?"

"Yes, beautiful. We arrived at the hotel, since it was a courtesy hotel shuttle, we did not have to pay but gave him a tip of course.

The hotel was huge, with amazing landscaping and palm trees, so different from where we lived.

We checked in and took the elevator to the ninth floor. Our suite had two rooms which meant somebody was sleeping on the pull-out sofa. I was not volunteering for that."

Angelina found that funny and turned her head to smile at me.

"Luckily, Tony volunteered. There was a fruit basket waiting on a table. At first, we thought it was courtesy of the hotel, then Bill read the card and said it was from the airlines. Apparently, the young lady who checked us onto our flight liked one of us, but it was not clear which one. It was very thoughtful of her and we enjoyed the fruit very much.

We all settled in and unpacked our bags once again. We changed into our swim trunks and headed for the pool.

Even though it was brutally hot and humid we found three chairs together and ordered some drinks from the waitress.

We did not have our drivers' licenses with us since we would be swimming, so she took our word for it that we were of legal drinking age, which we all were.

We were all sort of quiet, just enjoying the pool and awesome drinks, but I could not stop thinking of Keri, she was the only thing on my mind.

It was only maybe an hour since I had kissed her goodbye and watched her walk away, but it felt like forever. I wondered if she had even boarded her plane yet.

She said her flight was direct and she would be home in 3-4 hours. I left my cell phone in the room; afraid the heat would damage it.

As I laid back on the chair, I relived our last moments together, but it was too sad, so I had to rewind back to our time on the ship, walking, talking, swimming, eating, laughing, and enjoying each other.

As the intense sun baked my body, I was smiling. Her effect on me was something I had never experienced.

There were a small group of girls at the pool around our age and somehow Bill invited them over to meet Tony and I. We engaged in normal conversation, where we all lived, what we did for a living. This time there were three girls, well a younger sister who tagged along, making it four. Unlike on the cruise where we seemed to only meet pairs of girls.

But I was not interested in meeting any new girls at all. My mind was only focused on Keri.

I soon excused myself and headed up to the room, immediately checking my phone. I missed a call from a number I did not recognize, and it was not Keri's home number that she gave me. I quickly checked my voicemail, and a wave of comfort came over me, it was Keri's beautiful southern voice calling to leave me a message using her father's cell phone, letting me know her plane was delayed, and she would call as soon as she got home as planned.

After the guys came back up and we were all showered and dressed we left and headed out for the evening.

We got some advice from the young lady working the front desk regarding nearby restaurants and night clubs.

Honestly, I was not into going out and trying to enjoy myself when I could only focus on Keri. But I wanted my friends to enjoy this time, especially since they were not as lucky to have found a dream girl on the cruise."

Once again Angelina smiled at me.

"We had dinner at a cool little Mexican grill, and I tried my very first margarita."

"What's that?"

"An alcoholic drink. Incredibly good.

After dinner we strolled along the busy streets. It was exciting. People were happy, laughing, everyone seemed to be having a great time. Perhaps all vacationing as well.

We passed several clubs, but they did not appeal to us until finally one got Bill's attention. Perhaps it was the blaring music transcending through the walls or the attractive women entering, so we decided to check it out.

We stayed for a while and had a decent time. I did not want to be the party pooper, but they understood I wanted to get back to the hotel and talk to Keri.

I insisted they stay and have fun, but they were ready to call it a night. So, we left and headed back to the hotel, stopping along the way to get a pizza as a late-night snack for the room.

As soon as I got into our room I headed for my bedroom and checked my phone. It was almost midnight, guess I lost track of time, and sure enough I had two missed calls from Keri's home number.

I listened to both voice messages. She was hoping I would call her back tonight but said she was tired and afraid she would fall asleep.

I did not care how late it was, I needed to hear her voice. I called and after several rings she answered. It was a sign of relief to hear her voice.

We talked for over an hour, and I knew my cell phone bill was going to be awfully expensive next month, but I did not care, it was worth it.

"Why would your cell phone bill be higher than normal, didn't you have unlimited minutes?"

"Well, back in the OLD days." We laughed.

"They didn't have plans like they do today, and you paid like $.50 cents per minute. So, bills got pretty expensive."

"Regardless of an expensive phone bill we made a plan to talk each night I stayed in Miami."

"And when you went back home, did you still talk every night?

"We tried to. At first it was great, but then she was going off to college and would go back home every other weekend."

"Didn't she have a phone at college?"

"I don't think she had a cell phone. Her dorm room had a landline, but she shared with another girl, and that girl always seemed to be there when I called, and I would leave a message with her. They kept track of messages on a small whiteboard kept near the phone, but Keri would only get my messages on occasion. We would send letters and talk when she was at her parents' home, but life was busy for both of us.

She had to dedicate time to college and still worked a part time job."

I stared ahead at nothing, just reflecting on all the details I remembered about our brief relationship.

"And I was now getting ready to begin working at the agency which would change my life forever."

"Why grandpa?"

"Well, I had to move which was a big adjustment, then immediately begin months of vigorous physical, mental, and academic training, which was usually six days per week. Things with Keri just seemed to slowly disappear."

"Grandpa that's sad. I don't understand why."

"I couldn't keep my old cell phone. I was issued a new one with a new number. I called Keri a half dozen times at least, she was always in class or at the library, but each time I gave my new number to her roommate and asked that she write it down, so Keri got it. Still, I never got a call from Keri. I continued to send letters to her parents' home which I knew she would get when she visited them a few times a month and during semester breaks. I included my new PO Box address on the envelope and even wrote it again in my letter, just to make sure she had it.

In my letters I would tell her I had a new job working as an accountant with the Federal Government and had to move to Virginia. I could not tell her or even my family what my real job was, so my front for the time was an accountant and I would never

86

specify an agency or department, just simply, the Federal Government."

"What do you mean by front?"

"Sort of like a façade. Partially true. The Federal Government has many agencies and departments, I wasn't being specific, just generalizing."

"But grandpa how did you not tell your parents, family, and friends what you were really doing?"

"For many reasons, but mainly because friends and family would always have questions, and everything is confidential and a matter of national security."

"When did you finally tell my dad?"

"When we sat him and your aunt Emery down to let them know grandma and I were going to divorce."

I could see sadness come over her face and knew I had to get away from that topic, but she still had a few questions.

"We had to let them know that it was mostly because of my job and the strain it has put on our marriage over the years, and never once being able to discuss my work with your grandmother. It was not an easy life as I have told you before. Most couples can come home from work and vent to each other, I was never able to do that. Your grandmother felt like she was not even a part of my life. I was only home a few days a month, sometimes more."

"So, grandma knew what your job was?"

"Yes, but I couldn't even tell her until after we were married."

"Was she shocked?"

I laughed a bit.

"Yes, she was. She always had a lot of questions leading up to me telling her the truth. Like, if I were an accountant, why couldn't I at least work in a federal building closer to home, and so many more questions."

"So, to get back to the story. Eventually I just never heard from Keri again, so I stopped writing her letters and leaving her messages."

"So strange that she never wrote back to you or returned your calls."

"That's what I thought. I assumed she just found a new guy and moved on."

"But she could have at least let you know, right?"

87

"I agree."

"And that was it grandpa? You never heard from her again?"

"Never."

"That is a really sad ending."

"It was. But you know what, work had me extremely busy, so my mind was very occupied and eventually thoughts and questions about Keri seemed to fade."

"Has any other girlfriend stayed on your mind like Keri has for all this time?"

I stared at the wall for a moment and thought about her question.

"No."

"Hey, we should get ready for bed, we have another fun day tomorrow and we should get an early start to fully enjoy it."

"OK grandpa."

She got up and gave me a hug as I remained sitting.

"Goodnight."

"Goodnight angel."

As soon as I got to my room, I immediately checked social media to see if the last two Keri's responded. The internet connection was slow as I waited for the app to load, my mind was racing, and I was becoming anxious.

The app finally loaded and neither had responded. I convinced myself that no response was better than a negative response.

I hung my new dress on a hanger in the closet and then laid my jewelry and new bracelet on the nightstand.

After changing into my pajamas, I laid in bed. I said a prayer and asked God to let one of these two ladies be the Keri I am seeking and for things to work out perfectly.

Chapter 20

I have never discussed Keri with another person. I find myself becoming more curious about her now since reliving my time spent with her so many years ago, these last few days with my granddaughter. My training has taught me to easily turn emotions, feelings, empathy, sympathy, and even relationships on and off very quickly with hardly any remorse. But I now find myself trying to tunnel through these hardened walls and once again deliberate from my heart,

In this stage of my life am I ready for any sort of relationship with another woman? Am I too closed off emotionally? I am now interested to know where Keri is in her life but am I ready for another let down. What if she is still married and having a wonderful life? My deeply hidden desire to connect with her again would be shattered and condemn any hope I may have had to someday reunite with her.

Perhaps I will reach out to a handler friend and see what he can find out about Keri.

I made my way to the bedroom and got into bed, turned off the bedside lamp and drifted off to sleep.

Chapter 21

I woke at 8am to my phone alarm and after hitting snooze twice I decided to climb out of bed. The mattress and sheets were extremely comfortable which did not make it any easier getting up.

Before showering, I walked out of my room to see if Angelina was awake. I could hear her music playing at an exceptionally low volume as I approached her door.

"Angelina, are you awake?" I asked, knocking twice on the door.

"Yes."

"I'm going to shower and get dressed. Then we can go into town and check things out."

"Sounds good I will do the same."

I would later learn that the last two Keri's have still not responded.

When I came out of my room Angelina was sitting there on the big sofa waiting for me.

"Are you hungry?" I asked.

"Starving, but I did have an apple."

I smiled at her as I put my shoes on.

"I'm so hungry." I responded.

"Let's go." I said walking towards the door.

I noticed she did not seem her happy self.

"Everything OK." I asked.

She looked at me as if I were reading her thoughts.

"I'm fine, still waking up." She said smiling up at me.

Nothing got past my grandfather. He could read me like an open book. He knew something was troubling me but did not want to pry it out of me.

We walked down the hall and took the stairs to the first floor and made our way to the lobby. Most of the guest were wearing robes and had pleasant smiles for us as we passed them.

I went over to the concierge desk and asked if he could arrange a shuttle to bring us into town. He made a quick call speaking softly in Italian and then assured me it was taken care of.

Angelina and I walked over to a small table of refreshments and helped ourselves to a few small cartons of orange juice.

Before we could even take one sip the driver walked in and the concierge motioned to us that the driver was there.

I thanked the concierge and handed him a tip, which he appreciated.

The driver spoke English and asked us where we wanted to go.

"Just into town, near the marketplace. We are looking to have some breakfast before the shops open."

"Va bene, (OK)If you would like I could recommend an amazing little place that has the best breakfast in town."

"Excellent, drop us off there."

We could have had a wonderful breakfast at anyone of the several cafes throughout the hotel complex, but to me, it would be a much better experience to eat with the locals and the food is always amazing, besides, it would be a more fun experience for Angelina.

We passed by the market area and it was noticeably quiet as only a few merchants were bringing their goods back to the tents.

Angelina just stared out of the window taking in this incredibly old beautiful town.

The driver soon slowed down and pulled over to the curb.

"Here we are signore."

I already had a bill in my hand to give the driver and slipped it to him.

"Grazie." I said, as Angelina and I got out of the small shuttle van.

The driver then extended his hand back to me presenting his hotel business card, which I took.

"Signore, I'm on duty until 4pm, call me when you are ready to go back to the hotel."

"I will call you, thanks again."

He pulled away from the curb and drove off.

"It's cute grandpa." Angelina said, nodding her head.

"Sure is, now let's go eat."

Many of these small establishments are owned and operated by family alone which is great because they go above and beyond to make your food and experience the absolute best. They take pride in their work, service and products. Having owned several small businesses over the years myself, and now the winery, I can totally relate.

The pace in European countries is typically slower than in the states but I have become accustomed to it now and have grown to appreciate it.

We were greeted by a young lady who escorted us to a small table which overlooked a garden.

There were maybe 10 tables and six were taken now. The menu was only one sheet, and Angelina and I knew what we were getting with just a glance.

A simple menu makes ordering much easier and quicker.

The waitress brought our drinks and the large mug of coffee smelled so good and dwarfed the small glass of apple juice for Angelina.

She took our order. We both chose omelets, potatoes and toast. I could see pastries and muffins in a small glass case enclosure near the counter and walked over to see what the variety was.

I motioned for Angelina to come over and look, to see if she wanted one.

"I'm good grandpa, don't want to ruin my appetite before breakfast."

"I'm getting a muffin and a pastry." I said with a laugh.

The waitress saw me looking and came over to see if I wanted anything.

I pointed to the two I wanted, and she put them both on a small plate and brought them over to the table.

Angelina gave in and had half of the lemon danish. I noticed her glancing at her phone every few minutes, as if she were anticipating a message or something quite important to her. Having an intelligence officer for a grandfather has never seemed to phase Angelina, especially at her young age. Unfortunately, I am not able to turn off the skills I have learned over the years, they have become instinctive for me. Everywhere I go, every room I enter, I am assessing and evaluating the entire situation. Even as I sit here enjoying breakfast with my granddaughter I can tell you the number of tables, how many people are at each table, from my trip to the bakery display case I can tell all but two guests are from neighboring countries simply by their accents, that there are two exits, both very easy to access, that the woman behind the counter is the mother of our waitress just by the sense of affection they display towards each other, and that the mother is not married due to lack of a wedding band and no tan line on her finger, that there were two cars parked outside indicating most guests are staying at nearby hotels or resorts, and that my granddaughter seems troubled and concerned about something but I don't want to continuously ask questions and make her uncomfortable.

These instincts have saved my life, the lives of others, and helped keep my loved ones safe over the years, but these same instincts can sometimes make life wearisome.

Chapter 22

We finished our meals and were eager to enjoy the sites, shopping, and peaceful daytime environment.

As we strolled along, the merchants began to reopen their stores slowly. Delivery trucks started rolling in and the store owners were more than happy to see them. They all seemed to know each other as they greeted one another using first names. The fresh baked goods smelled delicious as they were carried from the small trucks into the stores that sold food as well as the small cafes along our walk.

I was never much of a shopper, just always getting what I needed and not consumed with collecting items or even clothing just for the sake of buying. But I enjoyed watching Angelina shop, it reminded me so much of my daughter when she was that age, girls just seem to take much more pleasure with the whole shopping scene.

The marketplace was not excessively big, and much quieter during the day. We came upon a small stand set up outside of a shop. Just a table with a teenage girl sitting on a chair looking very bored. I could tell by the supplies on the table that she offered nail painting.

"Hey, would you like to get your nails painted?" I asked, pointing to the stand.

"Sure!"

We walked over and the young girl greeted us with a big smile, happy to just have a potential customer.

Angelina picked out the color and the young girl immediately went to work, within a few minutes all ten fingernails were painted a lovely violet color.

I gave the girl double her price and told her it was a tip for being so good and so professional. The girl's mother stood at the shops doorway and thanked us as well.

Angelina did not really find anything she wanted to buy and told me what she got last night was plenty.

So, we decided to take a taxi back to the resort and enjoy the beautiful, heated pools and jacuzzi.

As usual, most guests were roaming around in robes holding drinks admiring the artwork and sculptures while casually socializing.

We took an elevator up to our floor and had the hall to ourselves as we made our way to the room. We immediately changed into our swimsuits and of course our robes and just as quickly left. I noticed a smile upon Angelina's face when she came out of her bedroom and I decided to comment on it as we made our way to the elevator.

"You seem happier."

"I've been happy grandpa."

"I know, but you seem even happier, I'm glad."

We arrived at one of the pools, as Angelina sat down, I could see her tapping away on her phone.

"I will meet you in pool."

"OK grandpa, be right there."

There were only thirteen guests in this pool area including Angelina and I. It was beautiful, Romanesque style décor, amazing granite and marble sculptures and tables, complete with stonework steps leading into the water at several locations. The pool wasn't meant for laps, it was very large, with several small little cove areas, with built in underwater stone benches where couples or small gatherings could have some privacy, while soaking in the 90-degree water, which varied between four feet and five feet in depth.

Angelina had finished up her texting and was now swimming over to me. I was sitting on a small stone bench in the water just big enough for two people, situated next to a waterfall, which Angelina swam under as the water completely drenched her head while she laughed.

"Grandpa this is so beautiful, and the water is like a bath. I took a few photos to send to mom and dad."

Just then a waiter came by and knelt beside us on the deck.

"Would you care for some beverages?" He said with a very pleasant smile.

"Would you like anything?" I asked Angelina.

"Sure, do you have lemonade?"

"Absolutely!" The waiter replied.

"And I will have a glass of your Bardolino."

"Excellent!" He replied, and then slowly walked away.

Our second night here would be more relaxed for Angelina. No friend joining us, no business to discuss, just a relaxing and quiet evening while enjoying this wonderful experience.

We spent this time moving between the pool and the 10-person jacuzzi, which we both enjoyed. At any given time, there were less than four people in the jacuzzi and maybe a dozen or so in the pool, so that was quite nice.

Angelina was not very hungry, so we decided to skip lunch and visit the pool area on the other side of the spa. It was about a 12-minute walk along the beautiful pathway that took us through several flower gardens, numerous areas that had lounge chairs for sunbathers as well as small intimate settings with tables meant for two, and larger tables that could seat six. A manmade stream ran along most of the pathway complete with several small waterfalls strategically placed to make this an experience rather than simply passing from one pool area to the other.

It was such a beautiful day, 82 degrees, sunny and hardly any humidity. Angelina and I were already very tan from the time we spent outdoors and enjoying our own pool back home, but we still wanted to experience this tranquil setting, so we found two lounge chairs as we entered the second pool area.

It was as equally impressive as the one we just left and had about the same number of guests.

As soon as we sat down a waitress came over and asked if we would like any refreshments, so we each ordered lemonade and I ordered a fruit, cheese, and cracker platter for us to snack on since we were not having a regular lunch.

Angelina kicked off her flip flops and sunk into the thick, soft cushion of her lounge chair and began checking her phone.

Keri:

"Hi Angelina...I am the Keri that knew your grandfather so many years ago. It is hard to believe he is a grandfather, but I am a grandmother as well.

And yes, we did meet on a cruise when I was just 18 years old. How is he? I would love to hear more. Does he have an account on this site? I have searched for his name many times over the years but never found him. He is lucky to have such a granddaughter as you. I look forward to hearing back from you!"

~Keri

Angelina:

"Keri...OMG I am so happy to hear back from you. I was beginning to lose hope. Yes, you are really the Keri I am looking for. My grandfather is doing great. He has two granddaughters, me and my cousin, she is 8 and I am 12. He doesn't use social media at all, but he told me the story of you two meeting, and I know he has never forgot about you, that's why I reached out to all the Keri's with the same name, hoping the right one would respond, and you did! Thank you!"

Keri:

"He told you the story of us meeting on that cruise all those years ago. Why do you feel he has never forgot about me? Is he still married to your grandmother? If my memory serves me right, he should be around 60 years old right?"

Angelina:

"Yes, he has a box full of postcards and he lets me pick one out, then he tells me the story behind it. I found an envelope on the bottom of that box, and it had just stuff between you two, like pictures from the cruise, postcards of the ship, and letters that you wrote to him. He and my grandmother divorced way before I was even born, like 19 years ago, I think. OMG he is 60, how can you know that? Amazing! Are you married Keri?"

Keri:

"He kept my letters and pictures? So, touching! I am sorry to hear he has been divorced for so long. He was a very good-looking man; I am sure he has somebody now. I remember he was five years older than me, and I am now 55. You mentioned he never forgot about me, why do you say that?"

Angelina:

"Because he told me he has never forgot you, and never stopped thinking about you. Are you still married?"

Keri:

"I'm no longer married either. My husband passed away a few years ago. I have two children and one grandson. I must run right now; I have an appointment. I would love to learn more about your grandfather. Does he have any idea you searched for me? If not,

maybe you should not tell him just yet. I would love to talk to him. Let's chat a bit more later. I will message you."

Angelina:
"That would be great. No, he has no idea I searched for you and he might get upset, I hope not. I did this behind his back. I am sure he would love to talk to you as well. I can't wait to hear from you later."

Angelina:
"Keri wait, please! Your profile says that you live in Florida. We are in Italy and there is a huge time difference, you are 6 hours behind us."

Keri:
"Italy! Sounds wonderful. I will message you after my appointments, like 4pm my time, so 10pm Italy time. Can you stay awake?"

Angelina:
"YES!!! Thank you!"

"Angelina. You are so caught up in that phone you did not even notice that the waitress has brought our drinks and this food. Have some grapes or something."

"I love you grandpa!"

"I love you too my little Angel. What prompted you to say that?" I smiled as I sipped my drink.

"Just because."

"That's good enough for me."

There is nothing quite as wonderful, as hearing those words from my granddaughters.

She looked so happy, whatever may have had her a bit upset was now replaced with joy.

We picked away at the sampler platter of various fruit slices, several different cheeses, crackers, and bread.

"This is paradise grandpa!"

"It sure is."

It is nice to be at a place in my life when I feel I do not need to be on guard 110% of every minute of every hour of every day.

The instincts that I have developed over the years will always be a part of me, it is who I am, and I am very thankful for that. But the fact that I am no longer in the field gives me a slight sense of peace.

I do not have to run surveillance detection routes every time I drive home, have meetings in strange locations, visit someone at their home or hotel all hours of the day and night, or even just meeting up at a restaurant or diner to discuss work related details.

This entire complex is gated, security is very tight, but over the years I have made many enemies, and if you are on somebodies list, there is nothing that can prevent them from reaching you, I know from experience.

More important than my own life, is the life of my beautiful granddaughter lying next to me. For these reasons, I am always prepared, and thankful for the instincts and skills the agency has instilled in me.

I never leave my home without at least one weapon. Besides years of hand-to-hand combat training to rely on, I always have weapons. And what I may not be carrying on me, I am assessing and evaluating every place I go, every room I enter, immediately looking for items that may be used as a weapon if a struggle suddenly broke out. Not many people have this mindset, and they will be the ones completely surprised and caught off guard should a sudden crisis occur. I have experienced too many of these situations over the years.

"Let's try out this pool grandpa!"

"Let's do it!"

One thing is for sure, spending all this time with a 12-year-old, helps to keep this old body in shape.

This pool had a similar shape as the other one but with minor differences. Instead of just staircases leading into the water, there was a ramp on the far end, which was nice because it allowed access for handicapped people.

So, we entered by way of beautifully carved stone steps and immediately immersed ourselves into this warm crystal-clear water. There was no odor of chlorine so they must use an alternate like I do in my pool.

Without a doubt Angelina was the youngest guest at this resort. Most guest were closer to my age, except for several in their 30s or 40s.

Everybody kept to themselves except for the occasional nod, smile, or wave while passing.

We casually made our way around the entire pool, careful not to disturb some couples who were kissing while tucked away in little private coves. I cannot blame them, this is a very romantic and charming resort, and this pool area was incredibly tranquil.

When we reached the other side, we walked up the ramp, it was about ten feet wide so even if passing people there was still plenty of room. We each grabbed a towel from the crate holding them at the edge of the ramp before walking back to our table and chairs. Angelina wrapped her large plush towel around her body as I just patted the water from my face.

Our plate was still there with little left to be eaten but our glasses were missing. I could see the waitress heading our way to ask if we would like another drink or anything else from the kitchen.

We both decided on a drink, Angelina settled on a raspberry lemonade while I had a glass of my vineyards wine.

We just simply relaxed, soaked in the sun and ambiance as we sipped on our drinks. I checked my phone for any messages or missed calls. Isabella handled the calls and emails for the business through an upgraded system I had installed for her in the Martone home, it was very convenient for her, and I would not need anyone inside my home. I know if anything of importance should arise, she would call me or email me.

Angelina did not seem so concerned with her phone as it remained under her dry towel. She did not even have her earbuds connected listening to her own music, instead she listened to songs in Italian being quietly piped through hidden speakers placed throughout the resort, as she tapped her fingers on her armrests.

Chapter 23

After several hours in the warm sun, we both decided to go back to the room and take showers then get ready for our last evening.

I directed our route so that I could show her two other restaurants the resort offered, giving her the choice, so we could try something different this evening.

Angelina liked the menu choices of a less casual restaurant as the previous night. So, we finished looking at the menu then we scanned the interior, and both nodded in agreement. It had more enthusiastic music, soft lighting, high top tables for two, but also tables for 6-8, and cozy small private booths along the walls for those seeking more intimate dining.

I would prefer the private booth, but Angelina loved the high tops situated along the windows especially since she is a people watcher and loves to admire women's clothing. Europeans have somewhat different styles than that in the US, which intrigued her. She loved looking at the various dresses, and expensive jewelry most women were wearing, and did it in a such a way that it was inconspicuous and even if a woman saw Angelina glancing, they would just smile back in a pleasant way. She also enjoyed the variety of languages spoken by the different guests, as I would try to figure out which language it was just by listening to a few brief words in passing.

I approached the hostess and made a reservation for 5pm, which allowed us enough time to shower and rest in our room before dinner. I also asked for a specific high top which would allow me to have my back to a wall and allow Angelina a nice view of people passing by.

As usual the hallways were quiet, we only passed a few guests, then we slipped into the stairwell and made our way up to the room.

I handed the keycard to Angelina and without her even noticing I glanced to make sure my marker was still in the same location of the door jam, as she swiped the card and the door unlocked. We entered, I picked it up, and placed it next to the card key Angelina laid on the small table near the entrance.

She picked a few grapes from the fruit basket as she walked by heading to her room.

"I'm going to shower and get ready for dinner grandpa."

"OK me to."

I checked my phone to see if I had any missed calls or text messages, there were none.

After showering, I could hear Angelina speaking loudly from her bedroom. I put my robe on and walked out to get a bottle of water from the refrigerator.

She must have been on a video chat with her parents as I heard a male and female voice. Just then Angelina swung open her door and was a little startled to see me standing there holding a water bottle.

"Grandpa! I was just coming to get you; mom and dad want to say hi."

I personally do not like video chats, but over the years I have had many with my grandchildren, so I have adjusted a bit.

Her laptop was situated on a small table with a chair which has been temporarily transformed into a mini desk area as Angelina had all her devices and cords perfectly set up and charging.

As I came into view, I waved.

"Hi dad!" My son and daughter in law both said simultaneously and waving back.

"Dad you are really spoiling this little girl."

"Well, I have nobody else to spoil, and plus she is excellent company."

"Thank you for letting her come stay with me, she is truly a breath of fresh air."

"Of course, dad."

"And now she wants to move to Italy, and I am 100% in favor of that!" Marla commented while laughing.

"Angelina said the resort is absolutely beautiful!"

"It so is mom, it's paradise!"

I just smiled and enjoyed the exchanges between the three of them, occasionally chiming in here and there.

"Well, I am going to get ready for dinner, our reservation is fast approaching. So nice talking to you both, Angelina is wonderful, I love having her with me and appreciate her company so much. She will not want to go home in a few weeks."

"No, she won't dad. Thanks again for having her, enjoy the resort, talk to you soon."

"Bye Marla."

"Bye dad."

"Bye Vincent."

"Take care dad, talk to you soon."

I gave the seat back to Angelina who was just leaning on the table next to me.

I could hear them saying their goodbyes as I closed the door behind me.

Chapter 24

I was sitting in the living room watching a local news station when Angelina walked out of her bedroom.

She looked so beautiful wearing the new dress she picked out last night. She styled her hair in such a way that it accented her earrings.

I turned off the TV and raising from the sofa I smiled at her.

"You look beautiful my little angel! You made the right choice with that dress."

"Thank you, grandpa." She replied as she hugged me.

"Are you ready?"

"I'm starving!" She quickly replied.

We left the room, and I slipped the marker into the door jamb without Angelina even noticing, then we casually made our way to the elevator. We would be a few minutes early so there was no real sense of urgency.

As we arrived at the restaurant, as always, I held the door for Angelina, as the same hostess immediately greeted us.

"Good evening, we have your table waiting for you." She said, smiling at both Angelina and me.

"Thank you." I replied.

I took the seat I had planned on with my back against the wall, as I nonchalantly assessed the surroundings.

We had a very nice young lady as our waitress who quickly took our drink order, as we glanced at the menu once again, even though we pretty much had already decided what meals we were getting. So, I took this time to decide on an appetizer that we could both enjoy.

Angelina loved the lemonade in Italy as almost all of it, especially in resorts, private restaurants and eateries made it using fresh lemons grown right in this country.

I of course was having a glass of my wine.

Since this was a more casual restaurant, most dishes were from the grill.

Angelina and I have similar food preferences.

She chose marinated grilled chicken with brown rice and sauteed carrots. I went with a larger meal of marinated grilled steak and chicken, along with brown rice and carrots as well. For an appetizer we both agreed on sauteed grilled shrimp.

As we enjoyed the fresh baked bread, we discussed the day's events. Angelina told me she is looking forward to going back home tomorrow so she can spend time with Lucia. She knows she will be returning home in a few weeks and I can tell a part of her is already feeling sad.

Only the adult Martone children have cell phones, so Angelina cannot even text Lucia.

The lighting in here was incredibly low, and the tables and booths spaced far enough from each other so that guests had adequate privacy. Angelina especially loved the little lights strung along the ceiling that gave the illusion of stars.

"So, what would you like to do after dinner? Do you want to go back to the marketplace? Or just relax around here?"

She fumbled with her straw a bit, poking it into her drink as she pondered the question.

"Maybe we can just stay here grandpa if that's ok."

"Of course, it's ok."

"Maybe we can walk that same trail, from one pool to the other. I bet its really pretty at night with lights."

"Sounds great."

We enjoyed the delicious grilled shrimp as our meals arrived shortly after and smelled amazing. The meat was still sizzling in the cast iron bowls.

"Be careful, those bowls are really hot." The waitress noted as she placed them in front of us.

"Grazie!" *(thank you!)* I responded.

"Prego!" *(you're welcome!)*

"Would you like more drinks?"

"Yes, please." I replied.

"This looks so good."

"Smells so good to."

Angelina nodded her head in agreement as she tossed the chicken and rice together. The carrots were in a separate cup.

We ate dinner while making small talk and enjoying the beautiful Italian music playing in the background.

When we were finished the waitress allowed us to sit and relax before asking if we were interested in dessert and coffee.

It is not like back in the states where dinners and meals are rushed, one course after another. In Italy, and in most European countries I have visited these same customs are relevant. It is genuinely nice.

I am not sure if Angelina, at her age, appreciates this custom, but after many years of rushed meals and fast food, I certainly appreciate it.

Angelina shared some news with me that I have not heard yet. Her mother purchased her a sewing machine, and material, and she has been drawing up some of her own clothing designs and can now practice right at home. She told me that she was inspired by her aunt Emery. It was like hearing Emery tell me those same things when she was around this same age or even younger.

She has expressed to me several times how she loves drawing dresses and various clothing items, and she genuinely has a passion for it.

She told me her mom and Emery talk all the time and that my daughter Emery will help her and support her anyway she can.

I bolster Angelina, in the same manner as I have encouraged my own children, to follow whatever dreams they have and choose something in life that they love and never just consider it a job.

So, hearing the excitement in Angelina's voice made me incredibly happy and I told her she would need to show me some of her drawings.

Angelina needed to visit the restroom and I pointed her in that direction. It was a brief walk from our table, and I had clear vision of her path.

The waitress stopped by to check on us and I told her we were ready to see the dessert tray.

Timing was perfect, as Angelina reached our table the waitress was steps away with the tray of amazing desserts. She enthusiastically told us what each was along with a brief description. Angelina was not very hungry and settled for a small dish of lime gelato. I was quite full but could not resist the tiramisu.

We enjoyed our desserts as the waitress casually left the check on the edge of the table near me.

I opened the jacket the check was in as I removed the pen from my pocket. I wrote in the tip and signed.

"Grandpa how come you don't pay for things with cash or credit card around here. I notice you just sign the check. Is it somehow linked to our room?"

"Yes. When we checked in, they swiped my credit card. So, I just sign my name and room number for every expense we have then we will get an itemized bill early in the morning before checking out. I will review the bill for any discrepancies, if there are none, I will just tell them to leave all the charges on my card and that's how it works."

She just smiled back at me.

Both of us were now quite full as we made our way to the exit but not before saying good night to the waitress and hostess.

I led us in the direction of the first pool we swam at today. Strings of lights that were not visible during the day now sparkled everywhere, on the bushes, trees, along the fence, as the underwater pools lights gave off an aqua blue effect.

Several people were in the pool, enjoying conversation, sipping on drinks, while four others were in the jacuzzi.

We made our way along the path; it was lit up as well.

"What time is it grandpa?"

"It's 7:55pm."

"Thanks."

"Do you have an appointment?" I jokingly asked.

"No, just wondering." She said with a laugh.

We passed several couples walking the opposite way as we approached the other pool. It was equally lit up and decorated, only the underwater pool lights were almost a violet color.

Six people were in that pool and just two enjoying the jacuzzi. The restaurants all served food until midnight, so I am assuming these people had earlier dinner reservations or will possibly have late night dinners.

"Would you like to do anything else?"

"Maybe we can just go back to the room and put PJs on. I would love a story!"

"But we don't have the box, and I told you the whole story about meeting Keri."

"I hope you don't mind, but I brought a postcard I picked out before we left."

I turned to her with a surprised look.

"You did?"

"Yep!"

"I don't mind at all."

We continued walking until reaching our hotel. We then kept the same slow pace through the empty hallways as to simply enjoy the quietness. Both of us still feeling very full we decided to take the elevator and not the stairs this time.

As usual, I handed the key to Angelina to swipe as I glanced at the door jamb to make sure the marker had not moved.

She opened the door, and this time I caught the marker before it fell to the ground. Once inside, I disposed of it in the trash can.

"I'm going to put my PJ's on, and I will meet you on the sofa with the postcard."

"Sounds good, I'm getting into mine as well."

Chapter 25

Angelina was already on the sofa when I came out of my room. She had a big soft blanket covering her little body, while her phone and the postcard lay on a pillow next to her.

"Would you like a drink?"

"No, I'm good."

I poured myself a glass of the wine which left maybe one more glass in the bottle. I would finish that tonight because I do not believe in wasting good wine.

"Are you cold?"

"I'm a little chilly."

I walked over and checked the thermostat. It was on 68 degrees, so I raised it up to 70, then made my way to the sofa.

"Is there room under there for me?" I asked jokingly.

"Of course," She responded flapping the blanket over so I could cover my legs.

I took a sip of wine then placed the glass on the end table.

"Let's see what story you chose for this evening!"

She handed me the postcard. I stared at it for a few minutes as I gathered my thoughts, always keeping in mind I must give her the delicate version of the story.

The postcard was of the beautiful Galapagos Islands, in Ecuador. This was a very risky and intense clandestine operation

I held the postcard and began.

"Beautiful islands, and a beautiful country. This was a very secret operation. We needed to somehow penetrate a powerful drug lords' operation. It would be extremely risky. These guys do not play games. It is all business. They kill their own family members, so you can only imagine how ruthless they are.

It was a major drug cartel, and Ecuador is a leading cocaine superhighway into the US and Europe. We had recently received information they were also now transporting weapons, and those weapons were falling into the hands of ruthless gangs operating in the US. So now we had two problems, large quantities of drugs and arms being shipped into the US and Europe, one of our greatest allies.

We knew who the drug lord was, but there is no way you were penetrating his inner circle, so we came up with another plan. It would be very risky, but we needed to act swiftly because shipments were moving quickly.

So, a few of us brainstormed and came up with a plan. We had officers already stationed in Ecuador to gather critical information using miniature drones. The drones were very tiny and made to resemble a bee. We found out the drug lord and his inner circle spent most of their time tucked away in the mountains in a very camouflaged compound. This drug lord owned most of the rental properties on the islands and throughout many of the towns.

The drones were able to capture voice and facial recognition of him and his only brother. His brother was much more mild mannered. He had a finance degree and was not only was the drug lords right hand man, but, he also controlled the financial end, making all the investments and deals with major banks to launder money into many shell companies."

"What do you mean by launder money grandpa, and what are shell companies?"

"Basically, taking illegal cash from selling the drugs and guns, and paying banks a fee to deposit all that cash, then they can transfer that money electronically to various make-believe or shell companies which they own, and even transfer money to foreign banks throughout the world. Very similar to the paper companies I told you about before"

"So, it's all illegal?"

"Yes, it's all illegal."

"So now me and my team flew to Ecuador and began tracking the brother's movements. Each day he traveled to several banks, usually ate lunch at different restaurants, and made other miner stops along the way. He traveled with two bodyguards and they drove a large silver SUV with very dark tinted windows. But because of the heat, most vehicles had tinted windows, but there were only a few $80,000 SUV's driving around. Since I oversaw this operation, I decided we would stage a strong-arm robbery when the vehicle made

110

a stop at one of the banks which only had one armed security guard at the inner door.

Before leaving for Ecuador, I had our fabrication department make a small realistic gun that fired blanks, no bullets.

The bank security guard is trained to not leave the bank under no circumstances.

One of my guys would have the gun firing blanks only, and the other guy would have a real gun.

My two guys were waiting around the corner of the bank in a beat-up mid-size car, which blended in perfectly around this area, while I was inside the bank waiting to walk out as this plan came together. When the SUV pulled up, both bodyguards got out and opened the door, my guys ambushed them and immediately shot both bodyguards."

"They just shot them?"

"Yes, but only in the legs so they couldn't chase after them."

I did not want her to know they had to shoot them dead, or it would have been a showdown. This had to be quick and precise. No screw ups or loose ends.

"Just as my one guy was pretending he was going to shoot the drug lords brother, I rushed out of the bank and tackled him, my other guy with the fake gun pretended to shoot at me. Now, the fake gun is just as loud as a real gun, so everything appeared real. My two guys then took off in the car leaving me behind. This was the plan but also a huge risk for me."

I could see the intrigued yet worried look on Angelina's face

"By now the police had been called and the bank guard finally emerged to see of what assistance he could be now that the incident was over.

I had gotten up and asked the drug lords brother if he was ok. He was visible shaken as I helped him out of the vehicle. He glanced at his two bodyguards in horror. He kept staring at me as if he were confused as to why I helped him.

He finally spoke, in particularly good English, and asked if I was ok. I quickly examined my body and told him I appeared to be. Just then the police showed up along with an ambulance. Crime scenes there are not treated in the same manner as in the US. The two bodies were basically placed on separate stretchers and loaded into the ambulance and whisked away to the morgue I assumed.

111

The police immediately recognized the brother and greeted him as if he were the president. He proceeded to give the police his statement, as I searched for my briefcase that was thrown during the occurrence.

The bank guard was giving another policeman his take of the incident and I could see him pointing at me.

The plan seemed to be working perfectly.

The police never spoke to me directly. They were done questioning the brother, when he walked over to me and extended his right hand. I reached out and we shook. He told me I saved his life and he wanted to thank me. He took out a business card and told me to text him the street name as he pointed up to the sign, within one hour.

His card was quite simple. It had a business name, an investment company, then his name and a phone number.

He then got into the vehicle and drove away quickly. I immediately took out my cell, one that could be traced, not my ghost cell. I texted him the name of the street.

The police were now gone, the guard went back into the bank, and besides two small puddles of blood, it was as if nothing happened.

My two friends were waiting nearby in a newer car after ditching the older beat up one. When they saw the police had left, they came by to pick me up after I had walked several blocks from the scene.

We were all staying nearby, in Quito, the capital of Ecuador.

My cover for this trip was working as an environmental consultant for a large US company. The hotel room had been rented for the last 30 days under this company name.

Remember before I told you that my agency makes agreements with companies and they vouch for us as employees?"

"Yes, I do,"

"Every base needs to be covered because criminals like this drug lord would have me checked out if this was going to move ahead.

I waited and waited for a text back. It finally came four hours later.

The text read; *I would like to invite you to a party tomorrow evening as my personal guest. Let me know if you can make it and I will confirm your name on the guest list.*

I waited about fifteen minutes before responding.

I would love to come.

And I gave him my cover name for this mission.

"What was it grandpa?"

"Now you know I can't tell everything."

We smiled at each other and I continued.

"Within a minute he responded and confirmed. He also let me know I could not bring a guest.

I knew he was now having me checked out, as I was having his location checked out. It was a different location from the compound his brother spent most of his time. But this property came back as being owned by one of the cartels shell companies. It was on one of these Galapagos' Islands."

I held the postcard up and pointed to one of the islands.

"This mission was going exactly as planned, but these instances were just laying the foundation.

I would spend the next 24 hours memorizing my new character. I have imitated an environmental consultant several times and know enough about the position to carry on a conversation. We also had created a profile for my character and included that I was involved with martial arts and implanted various tournaments I participated in within several major search engines."

"But you did study martial arts grandpa."

"Yes, but by mentioning it in this character profile it would explain my willingness to step in and help the brother that day at the bank.

An hour before the party I received a text that said a car would be sent for me.

The text did not ask where I was staying. A sure hint they had me checked out."

Angelina's eyes widened a bit.

"So, as to not make anything look suspicious, I replied with the hotel name in which I was staying.

A simple, *thank you*, followed.

I was waiting in the hotel lobby and had several officers situated where we had eyes on all roads leading to the hotel.

I was dressed casually, a light sport coat, short sleeve button up shirt with just the top button open as to fit the part of a conservative businessman.

The car pulled up, and it was a spotless Lincoln town car, silver, tinted windows.

The passenger got out and walked into the lobby. I was the only one standing there and he approached me and mentioned my name.

I shook my head and told him it was me. With no words, he turned and walked back out of the lobby as I followed him to the car.

Now in a situation like this, things can go completely awry."

"What do you mean?"

Angelina does not understand the danger of these missions and that my life is literally on the line so much of the time.

"Well, if anything in my characters background didn't check out the way it should, they would suspect me of being a spy and most likely kill me."

"Grandpa!!"

"I'm here, so obviously things worked out well."

I smiled and put my arm around her pulling her close, as to comfort her of any worry.

"He opened the rear door and I got in. The driver asked if I was carrying any weapon. I reacted as if shocked he would even ask me. I replied no, I have no weapons. But I did have my tactical pen with me. I never leave without something. No words were said as we drove. The driver glanced at me through the rear-view mirror from time to time as I pretended not to notice while gazing out the window. I had a tiny tracking device that I slipped from my jacket pocket which had a pin at the base, so I was able to push it into the bottom of the passenger seat while pretending to tie my shoe.

The ride lasted 55 minutes until we arrived at the gates. They looked at least ten feet tall. There was a guard shack and as the gates opened two heavily armed guards looked at the driver and nodded. We drove in and continued down a long road. I could see the beautiful ocean ahead and a large complex of homes off to one side. The parking area was full of cars which was a relief because now I felt this was a legit party and not a set up.

We drove right up into a huge, four car wide circular driveway. I could see the brother coming around from a side entrance. The guards at the gate must have signaled his guest had arrived.

As we came to a stop, before I could even reach for the door handle, the passenger jumped out and opened my door.

I got out and the brother greeted me, this time with a hug and not a handshake.

This was an incredibly good sign.

We made small talk and approached an area that was set up with a metal detector and four armed guards. The brother said, *please*, as he motioned for me to walk thru. I removed the tactical pen from my inside jacket pocket, showed it quickly to the guards and dropped it into a small bucket, walked through without an issue. One guard removed the pen from the bucket, looked at me, as if noticing it was heavier than a normal pen, but unless you are familiar with this pen you do not know how it can be transformed into a weapon. The brother said a few words in Spanish very quickly and the guard immediately handed the pen back to me, and we continued.

This place was almost as beautiful as this resort, and had the ocean as its background, but that's a whole other story."

We both laughed.

"We walked directly towards his brother, who for the sake of this story we will now call Carlos.

I recognized Carlos immediately from the drone images we have. This was a big deal. I could have never met Carlos on my own. One thing I have learned over the years is that if you are not the kind of person who can easily connect with a drug lord you are trying to take down, you will most likely be killed.

I had to be on my A game 110%. Not one aspect of an intelligence officer could be revealed even for a second or I would be under suspicion.

Carlos was surrounded by a small group of men, and then many small groups were close by, gravitating in his vicinity.

As we approached, his circle opened, and he was staring directly at me. A very cold-hearted ruthless man no doubt. He and his brother both stood about 5'7" tall with slim builds. All eyes were now on us. There were other Americans there, but mostly Ecuadorians. I did not have much time to assess the entire situation because he was immediately bringing me to meet Carlos.

As we were now just a few feet apart, the brother spoke to Carlos in Spanish. I know bits and pieces of the language, but they spoke it so quickly it was hard to follow. Carlos listened to his brother but never took his eyes off me. The people surrounding him did not move, did not even raise their glasses to sip their drinks. It was intense, but I have been in similar situations enough times to play the part.

The brother then turned to me with a smile and said, *this is my brother Carlos*, as if extremely proud of his brother.

I extended my right hand to shake, but it just lingered for what seemed like minutes, were literarily just seconds, then Carlos opened his arms and hugged me. It was a tight hug and a bit uncomfortable for me because I am not used to hugging men. I could feel his hands clench me.

As we separated, he continued looking at me, his eyes much softer now.

Thank you! Thank you! You saved my brother's life.

His accent was thick and his English broken.

I just did what anybody would have done. I responded.

No, he said shaking his head. *It is not what anybody would have done.*

He then summoned a waiter standing nearby with a tray of shot glasses.

He offered me one, his brother one, and he took one.

Nobody spoke, nobody moved, it seemed like every guest, every employee froze in time.

We raised our glasses as he spoke.

To your bravery, and for saving my beloved brother!

The three of us tapped glasses and finished the shot in one gulp.

Then with a wave of his hand, the music immediately began playing, people began conversing and the party resumed.

I remained in this circle speaking with Carlos and his brother.

I had to now focus on my mission. To find out when the large shipments of weapons were being scheduled to ship. Which route would be used since there are potentially several. How were they being shipped? By truck, boats, or planes. And where they were being stored before being sold in the US.

Dinner was soon being served and I would be seated at the head table right next to Carlos and his brother.

I had noticed a beautiful woman who all the other women seemed to gravitate around. She turned out to be Carlos third wife. I was introduced to her by Carlos before dinner began, she sat right next to him.

I got the feeling from the level of comfort amongst the guest that these sorts of parties were a common thing.

During dinner I was questioned by Carlos and his brother regarding my work, and why I was in Ecuador, what I liked about Ecuador and why I just happened to be in that bank the morning or the incident.

It was not in a form of interrogation, but merely conversation.

I responded that I was there on business, working with the US embassy in conjunction with the Ecuadorian government regarding preservation of their beautiful treasure, the amazon jungle. This seemed to make them smile. Compliments go extremely far and benefit intelligence officers very much. Human beings by nature enjoy compliments and anything that can boost a targets ego is not off the table.

I made sure to compliment how beautiful this property was, but never to ask what line of business they were involved in. Carlos and his brother offered some information, that they were involved in investment corporations and real estate.

I acknowledged and then moved to a different topic so no suspicion would be raised by me asking questions.

I told them I was only there on a 90-day visa, to which I was informed I could stay as long as I wanted and if I needed to extend beyond that, they would arrange for it if my embassy couldn't. I then made it clear I was not a government employee, and that I worked for a private US company.

I knew that Mexican drug cartels had strong bonds with Ecuadorian mobs, and this is how drugs were moved from South America to North America, so my assumption was this is how weapons are being moved as well.

I also knew that Carlos was the most powerful mob boss in Ecuador.

Carlos was hard to read, but I could tell he accepted me. During dinner he asked if I liked scuba diving. I told him I had only been a few times but understand that the south pacific where these islands are located, had the most colorful marine fauna and amazing underwater cliffs and corals.

He and his wife both agreed. And seemed happy with my basic knowledge.

117

Part of my training is to learn and have a working knowledge of every situation and encounter I may experience during every mission. You must fit in.

You should come scuba diving with us sometime.

I would love that.

He then pointed to an area I had not looked at much, it was his private marina with many boats, but beyond that was a huge ship, almost resembled a smaller version of a cruise ship.

Is that yours? I asked him.

They are all mine, he said with a smile.

I gave a look showing how impressed I was.

Again, complement the ego."

Angelina smiled, and I noticed her check the time on the phone.

"Are you expecting a call or video chat?"

"No, just one of my girlfriends will be messaging me at 10pm our time."

I glanced at the time and decided to shorten up the story so she could communicate with her friend.

"You sure I'm not boring you?"

"Grandpa. You know I love these stories. Why do you think I even brought this postcard?"

Wait, was my granddaughter using a compliment and flattery on me, was I the target I just described to her during this story. I laughed out loud.

"What's so funny?" she asked putting her face right in front of mine.

"Nothing."

We both laughed and I continued.

"Carlos's wife had limited English, so she didn't speak much.

I was asked if I was married, and I responded with the truth, that I was divorced.

Carlos's brother chimed in that he was also divorced.

Commonalities with targets is also beneficial. It puts you on the same playing field.

As the hours passed, I began putting a slight version of the puzzle together.

Carlos mentioned he had a large project in the works that should be completed by the end of the month, in which only eight days remained.

At another point in the conversation, he mentioned he enjoys traveling a certain route by boat, because there is not much traffic.

At one point he dropped a bomb by telling me he owned a shipping container company as well that operated out of both major ports in Ecuador.

The shipping containers are placed on ships, travel into Mexico, off loaded and put onto tractor trailers and driven into the US.

At this point I feel I had a good working knowledge of this operation. It was now well into the evening, we all had a lot of food, and many alcoholic beverages.

I controlled mine so I was always in complete control of my bearings.

I thanked Carlos and his brother for having me and showing me such incredible hospitality during this visit.

Carlos summoned a bodyguard, which were spread out along the perimeter and walking around casually observing the guests and to make sure a level of comfort was kept.

He whispered into the bodyguard's ear which told me this guard was well trusted.

The guard then left and returned within a few minutes carrying a small briefcase and a giftbox.

Carlos and his brother both walked with me to an awaiting car, that would be my ride back to the hotel. Several bodyguards trailed behind.

They each hugged me and then Carlos presented me with the gift. I tried to refuse, but by his glance, I understood refusing a gift would be an insult. I opened the box, and this is what was inside."

I lifted my wrist and showed her the Rolex watch.

"Oh my God!" She gasped as she held and looked at the watch.

"I thanked him for the gift, and he told me to open the briefcase later, that is was another way of thanking me for saving his brother's life. He told me if I ever needed anything to call his brother and they would help in anyway.

I got into the car and we drove off. The whole time I wanted to open the briefcase. So many situations flashed through my mind. Was it a bomb? That was my biggest fear. I had to act natural and show no emotion, no fear. The same two guys who picked me up were now driving me back to the hotel. And as usual, the driver

119

glanced at me in the mirror several times. And once again, I pretended I did not notice.

I took a moment to remove the tracking device I placed under the seat earlier and slipped it back into my pocket.

Fifty-five minutes later we arrived at the hotel. The watch remained in the gift box and I gathered it and the briefcase while exciting the car as the passenger held the door open for me.

I thanked them both for the ride, and they simply nodded and drove off out of sight.

I made my way to the elevator and up to my floor. A sign of relief came over me, yet I was still in their country, and not out of danger yet. Glancing at the tiny piece of paper in my door jamb I could tell nobody had entered.

I quickly called my two officers and told them to convene in my room asap and bring equipment. One of them was a detection expert and I wanted him to examine the briefcase before I opened it.

They were on standby waiting for me and were at my door within minutes.

Several tests were run, and it was determined the briefcase was clean. Just then I received a text from Carlos's brother. He thanked me for coming to the party and told me he and Carlos were impressed with me and enjoyed my company. He also wondered if I liked the watch, then said he hoped I was not offended by the cash gift. He said Carlos is very generous and what I did could never be forgotten and deserved a gracious reward.

Before responding to the text, I asked my officers to leave and told them we would meet at the hotel bar in ten minutes.

I carefully opened the briefcase, and it had a very generous amount of US cash neatly packed inside.

I left the room and went to meet my coworkers and discuss everything that happened so we can act on the intelligence I obtained this evening."

"Was there a lot of cash grandpa." Her eyes widened.

"There was a good amount." I smiled back.

"So, what happened, did you stop the guns from coming into our country?"

"I did. Everything worked out well. We devised a well calculated operation to seize the containers as they entered Mexico. Then the proper law enforcement agencies seized the drugs and guns from this enormous shipment. But unfortunately, there are many Carlos's out there who are constantly shipping drugs and guns. But we do what we can to stop it."

"Your job was very scary and dangerous grandpa."

"At times." I said in agreement.

"You should write a book about all these stories someday grandpa."

"It's not that easy."

"Why? Just tell the stories the same way you tell them to me."

"The place I worked for wouldn't want these stories told." I said with a smile.

"I understand grandpa, but I still think they would make for an interesting book"

"Perhaps." I remarked with a grin.

I then noticed her checking the time again.

"Perfect timing, it's almost 10pm."

"Yeah, I'm going to go lay in bed and text my friend."

"Good night angel." I said placing a kiss on her forehead.

"Set your alarm for 9am so we can have breakfast before boarding the boat."

"Ok grandpa, goodnight!"

"Goodnight!"

Chapter 26

Angelina walked quickly into her room and closed the door behind her.

Her laptop I am sure was up and running and just needed to be refreshed.

Angelina:

"I am here Keri."

It was just 10:02pm, but I have been waiting all day to reconnect with this woman who captured my grandfathers' heart so many years ago.

Seconds seemed like minutes and minutes seemed like hours. Finally, at 10:16pm a faint *ding* sounded, and it was a message from Keri.

Keri:

"Hi, Angelina, sorry I'm running a few minutes late. So, your profile says CT, are you on vacation in Italy?"

Angelina:

"No problem I'm so happy we connected again. Yes, I live in CT with my parents, but spending a month of summer vacation in Italy with my grandfather. He lives here."

Keri:

"That is wonderful. Sounds like you two have an amazing relationship. I would love to connect with him and catch up. You mentioned he is not on any social media apps? If not, perhaps we can talk on the phone, I would love to hear his voice again."

Angelina:

"We really do have a great relationship; he is so wonderful. This is my second time visiting Italy to stay with him during my summer school break. Unfortunately, he is not on any social media, but we could definitely arrange a phone call. I just need to figure out how to tell him I searched for you and reached out to you."

Keri:

"We can figure that out. Does he work in Italy? I visited Italy years ago on vacation and fell in love with the culture and lifestyle. Can you send me a picture of your grandfather through our message chat? I would love to see his face again."

Angelina:

"Well, he is retired, but then he moved to Italy and bought a vineyard, so he runs that now. I love this place too. I don't have a photo, but I will take one in the morning and send to you ok?"

Keri:

"That would be wonderful! Wow he owns a vineyard in Italy, that is amazing. What was his career job that he retired from?

Angelina:

"It's such a cool vineyard, so big. There is a family that does all the growing, picking, and bottling, and my grandfather does all the paperwork and business side. He worked for the federal government for 30 yrs. Do you work in Florida and live there? Have you ever thought about my grandfather?

Keri:

"That sounds fantastic. I remember he had just graduated college when we met, and I had just graduated high school. Yes, I live in Florida, both of my children live in the state as well, not far from me, so I get to visit often. I run my own company as well. It may not be as exciting as a vineyard in Italy, but I love it. I started it years ago and have grown it into a lucrative business. To be honest, I do not think a day has passed that Anthony has not visited my thoughts and memories.

Those days on that ship with him were so magical. But I cannot help wondering why he just stopped writing to me and calling me. I would send him a letter and he just never responded, then he disconnected his cell phone so I could no longer even call him. I figured he found someone, perhaps your grandmother, and he went on with his life. That's the first question I am going to ask him when we talk."

Angelina:

"I don't know the story, but my grandfather told me that you just stopped responding to his letters and phone calls? That he would call your home and college dorm and send letters to your parents' home, but never heard from you again."

Keri:

"So strange, sounds like we both have the same story. Maybe he and I can get to the bottom of it when we speak. It has been a long day for me Angelina, I love messaging with you, but I need to fix dinner. So, you will take a photo and send it to me tomorrow? I also need you to tell your grandfather that you connected with me. Just be honest with him. And ask him if he would like to talk to me and catch up."

Angelina:

"I'm so happy I connected with you. Yes, I will take that photo in the morning and send it. I will also tell him what I have done and hope he does not flip out. Tomorrow we travel back to my grandfathers' home, we have been on vacation for a few days. So maybe he can call you then?"

Keri:

"Vacation for a few days sounds fun! He sounds like a cool grandpa; I am sure he will not flip out. Yes, he can call me anytime, but evenings work better. My home number is on my friends only page, and I have made you my friend. Have a great trip back home!"

Angelina:

"OK great, I wrote the number down. I will come clean on our trip back home LOL wish me luck!"

Keri:

"Good luck! It will be fine. Hopefully, he will be happy you found me and will want to talk to me."

Angelina:

"Oh, he will want to. I can tell he has missed you. Good night!"

Keri:

"You mentioned he retired from the federal government, what department did he work for?"

Angelina:

"Can you ask him when you talk. He's very private and I'm sure he would rather tell you."

Keri:

"Sounds mysterious LOL. Ok I was curious, my dad was in the military, which is part of the federal government."

Angelina:

"My grandfather was not in the military."

Keri:
"OK it will give us more to talk about. I am excited and looking forward to hearing from him. Good night!"
Angelina:
"Good night!"

Chapter 27

The night seemed to pass quickly and soon the sun was glaring through the large windows of my room. I could hear some rustling around outside my door and was surprised to find Angelina awake and dressed.

"Good morning Angel, you are up and about so early."

"I slept so good grandpa."

She was smiling from ear to ear.

"I showered, packed, and ready for the boat ride back home."

"Great!" I smiled. "You are a little ahead of me, relax while I catch up and we will leave very soon."

"OK!" She replied as she sunk into the comfortable couch with phone in hand.

I quickly shaved and showered. My clothes were already laid out on the bed and suitcase packed.

Before exiting the bedroom, I did a quick search just to make sure nothing was left in a drawer or the closet.

I yelled out for Angelina to do the same.

"OK I will double check."

I took my suitcase and small carry-on case which contained my laptop and other important files over to the door and confirmed with Angelina that she had left nothing behind while wheeling her suitcase over to the door.

To give me peace of mind and satisfy my OCD I had to double check Angelina's room. She stood by the door waiting. She did not question my actions. I am sure being around me for so many years she just accepts certain habits of mine, and I am incredibly comfortable with this silent acknowledgement and not having to explain my reasons.

"Are you ready?"

"Yes!"

With her backpack already on she took a hold of her suitcase and began pulling it down the hall as I locked the door and followed behind.

There was a middle-aged couple waiting for the elevator when we arrived. No words were spoken, just a smile and nod. The doors opened, and we allowed Angelina and the woman to enter first. Maybe I am a bit old fashioned, but chivalry was instilled upon me at a young age and will always be with me.

When we exited the elevators and walked towards the lobby, we both seemed to silently enjoy the sun shining on us through the windows of the halls. Everything about this resort is tranquil and instantly puts you in a good mood.

We walked up to the desk clerk and I told her our room number. She printed out the bill and it seemed to be much lower than I expected.

Before handing her my card I glanced over the charges and noticed our spa treatments and last nights dinner were all compensated for with the initials of the resort manager, next to each deleted charge. This was incredibly kind of him.

"Is Mario around?" I asked the clerk.

"Yes, would you like to speak to him?"

"Please."

She picked up the phone and within seconds of her hanging up Mario was walking towards us. His office is just around the corner.

Instead of a handshake Mario opened his arms, and although I am not a fan of hugging men, I had to be respectful and embrace him.

"Leaving us so soon? I hope you enjoyed your stay."

"It was just what we needed. This place is a dream. And thank you so much for your generosity Mario!"

"It was my pleasure Anthony. I hope to see you back here soon. And please, bring this, *bello signorina*." As he smiled at Angelina.

"I sure will. See you soon my friend."

We stopped at the concierge's desk and he called a taxi for us.

I slipped him a tip as we walked out to the waiting car. The driver placed the suitcases in the trunk, and we drove off to the harbor. Our boat is scheduled to leave in thirty minutes.

The roads were quiet this time of the morning and although I have loved this escape, I was looking forward to going back home.

The taxi dropped us off right at the dock and we walked along the old wooden planks to the beautiful boat taking us back home.

"Are you hungry?"

"Very."

"Me to. Let's get some breakfast and find a table for the ride so we can enjoy the sun and the sights."

"Sounds good."

I handed our tickets to the lady standing at the boats entrance, she glanced at them, then smiled at us.

"Welcome aboard!"

We both smiled back, thanked her, and made our way to the gentleman checking bags into the storage room. They basically tagged whatever luggage you did not want to cart around the boat and put it inside a large room next to the exit.

Once again, I checked in our two suitcases so we could easily move about the boat and not worry about bulky luggage, just her backpack and my small carry case.

We walked towards the dining area and I scoped out the exact same table we sat at during our trip here. Once again, there did not seem to be a large crowd, so finding seating anywhere seemed quite easy.

I liked this table because it was right near the railing and we would have an amazing view as we traveled back home.

Within seconds a waitress came over and greeted us as she laid out silverware and napkins.

"Can I start you off with some beverages as you look over the menu?"

I looked over at Angelina.

"Sure, I'll have orange juice."

"And I will have coffee and water please."

"I think I'm having scrambled eggs and toast."

"That sounds good." I remarked, as I continued looking at the menu.

The waitress returned with our drinks and we placed our order.

"Can I please have two scrambled eggs and wheat toast."

"Sure! And what would you like sir?"

"I will have a western omelet, wheat toast, and hash browns."

"Got it. Would you like hash browns as well?"

"Yes please." Angelina responded.

Just as the waitress walked away, the boat gently pulled from the dock, and we slowly drifted towards the middle of the lake before picking up a comfortable cruising speed.

I wanted to take a picture of grandpa and I, as soon as possible to send to Keri but doing so would not be that easy. My grandfather does not like his picture taken. So, I would have to soften him up a little with a compliment and then go from there.

"I like that shirt grandpa. We should take a picture together so I can show mom and dad."

Angelina knows I really do not enjoy having my picture taken. I am not a photogenic person. But she is so damn adorable how could I refuse.

"Let's take it leaning on the railing with the hills and water in the background."

She had her phone in hand and gestured for me to take it.

"You have a longer arm grandpa, so you take it."

I began laughing because I am not used to taking selfies at all.

We were laughing and did not notice the waitress refilling my coffee.

"Would you like me to take the picture?"

"Yes please!" Angelina exclaimed in relief.

The waitress took the phone and stepped back, as I put my arm around Angelina.

"Smile! Excellent! I took a few, they look very nice, let me know what you think."

Angelina took the phone and glanced at the photos.

"Thank you so much, they look great. Look grandpa."

"You look beautiful as always."

"You look great grandpa, I love it. I'm going to send it to mom and dad ok."

"Ok, and send me a copy also, to my email."

"Will do."

So, before our food came out, I sent the photo to both my mom and dad, and of course Keri.

Angelina:

"Hi Keri! I just took this photo of my grandfather and me. We are on a boat heading back home, to the vineyard. He does not like his picture taken, but I got him to. Hope you are having a great day, and I hope you like the photo!"

129

Breakfast was served and we began eating but all I was focused on was hearing the low buzz alert that I received a message.

Withing minutes my mother responded, telling me how jealous she is, wishing she were there in Italy with us.

At this point I knew I had to tell my grandfather what I have been up to. I could not let this linger on anymore. I found Keri and she is single and now wanting to talk to him. I am nervous. I do not want him to feel deceived by me in any way.

"Grandpa."

"Yes?"

"I can't stop thinking about your story with Keri."

He raised his eyes from his food and smiled, taking a split second from chewing.

"Why, out of all the stories I've told you, can't you get this one off your mind?"

"I guess it's because I cannot relate to most of the stories you tell me. They are scary and about your work. But this story, of you and Keri, is amazing. Like a movie. And what if you found her, and she is single to?"

"Angel, it's been 37 years. Don't you think she has a full life going on somewhere. Why get my hopes up only to be let down. She is still a young woman at 55. I'm sure she is married, has children, maybe grandchildren, a career, and who knows where she may even live, if she is even alive."

I could see sadness in his eyes, something I have never seen before. I had to seize this opportunity.

"I can't begin looking for her again, only to be let down. Sometimes our past is meant to stay right there. In the past."

"Grandpa!"

Once again, he took his eyes off his food to look at me. My body was tingling, like I was holding in a great secret, and did not know how to reveal it.

"What if the past isn't meant to stay in the past. What if I told you I found Keri on social media? What if I told you her husband died years ago and that she is single? What if I told you she is living in Florida? What if I told you I messaged her and we have communicated these last few days, and what if I told you she said not a day has passed that she hasn't thought of you since she last saw you on that dock in Miami."

After each, what if, I could see my grandfather's eyes lighting up, giving me his complete attention, focusing on every word coming out of my mouth.

There was a long pause that seemed like hours but was more like just a few seconds. I could feel my heart racing, anxious, nervous.

"Angelina. Tell me exactly what you are saying."

"I found the envelopes from the letters you and Keri exchanged all those years ago. I searched for her first and last name, hoping to come up with some clues.

Several women's names came up, and a few had hyphenated names, so I could tell they were married. I messaged each one and asked if any had met a man named Anthony on a cruise 37 years ago, then never saw him again and lost touch."

"Oh my God Angelina."

"All the women eventually responded. They wished me luck finding the right person. Yesterday, the real Keri responded."

I picked up my phone and opened the app, scrolling quickly until I opened Keri's page with her photo.

"Look grandpa, she is still just as gorgeous as when you two met."

I took the phone from Angelina and just starred at the photo. I felt a calming effect come over me as if a sign of relief, to see her once again. I had to remind myself to breathe.

Her eyes, her hair, her smile.

"She wants to talk to you grandpa. She has thought about you every day since you left that dock."

He glanced away from the phone to look at me. He smiled.

"You know, I may have a job for you at the agency when you get a little older."

We both laughed out loud.

"I sent her the photo we just took."

His eyes widened. He does not like any photos sent over any internet connection.

"Grandpa, she asked for a picture of you."

"So, you conned me into taking one. You are quite sneaky."

Angelina was laughing out loud now.

"But it was a nice picture of us."

"It sure is grandpa, and you look very handsome. I am sure Keri will think so. But remember, it's only like 5am in the states. My mom is a worry wart that is why she responded to the picture so

131

early. I'm sure she has her notifications turned way up in case I send her a message."

"So, you did all this just during our trip?"

"Yep."

"But you looked a little depressed or sad at times. Were you having any problems with friends back home?"

No. Not at all. It was because all, but two Keri's responded quickly letting me know they were not the woman I was looking for. My hopes were fading, I guess. It was down to just two, and of course the right Keri was the last one to respond."

She responded grandpa. I found her, and we had a great conversation, two of them, it's all right here if you want to read it.

I handed him my phone and he used his thumb to scroll down, reading the conversation quickly. My grandfather can scan and read more quickly than anyone I have ever seen.

He looked up at me again. His usual hardened eyes now seemed to have a softness.

"I hope you are not angry."

It took my grandfather time to respond as he glanced away from me and out at the water. Even at my age I know that he is never comfortable talking about feelings or emotions.

"No. Not angry at all. I'm actually relieved."

Angelina looked at me with a puzzled expression.

"Relieved because I have put this off for too many years. Ever since I found out she was married so long ago, I just sort of erased that thought from my mind. That one day we would reconnect and all those feelings we had from that cruise would resurface and we would spend the rest of our lives together."

He paused to sip his coffee then continued.

"Then I found your grandmother. We started our life together, and it just seemed like this was the direction life was taking me. Keri had her life in one state, and I had my life in another. We shared a brief moment in time. Distance separated us, and we were both too young to change that. But, like I have told you, she never has left my mind, my thoughts, or my heart. So, you did me a favor. You did the hard work for me."

"It wasn't really that hard grandpa. You could have easily done it."

"But if I did it, and found her, and saw that she was still married and had a family and maybe grandchildren, and her life appeared to be great....it would have taken the wind out of my sails. And I'm not just using that phrase because we happen to be on a boat."

We both laughed.

"So, by you doing the leg work without me even knowing, took the hard part away from me. For example, if you did this searching and Keri responded to you and said she was married and everything was great, you would have never told me right?"

"Right."

"So, you would have saved me from that depressing news, rather than me finding her and realizing that she was married, and her life was terrific. I had no plans to reach out for her because I wanted to avoid such hurtful news."

"Oh, now I get it."

I smiled at her, as it dawned on me that I was having such a deep conversation with my 12-year-old granddaughter, but strangely enough I was okay with it.

"So, I guess we will wait to see if she responds back or not after seeing the photo. I'm not 23 anymore."

"And she's not 18 anymore grandpa."

Once again, we found ourselves laughing out loud.

"But she still looks 18!"

"You both look amazing, and hopefully you will still have that same instant connection. I did my part grandpa the rest is up to you."

Still laughing so hard and tossing her arms up into the air.

I have a few regrets in my life, and one of the greatest is that my career consumed so much of my time. I feel I never had this close connection with my children like I do with Angelina.

Just then I could see the waitress approaching us.

"Would you two care for anything else? A refill perhaps?

"Yes please." Angelina responded.

"And I will take a refill as well, thank you!"

She smiled and took away our empty plates.

Glancing at my watch I was amazed seventy-five minutes have passed since we left the docks.

We both turned our chairs, to directly face the water and the amazing hills, with little towns nestled among them. A simple life

133

for most, unaware of what is really going on in this world, and better off not knowing.

The waitress returned and refilled our drinks. Angelina held her glass with the straw just touching her lips, and I sipped the hot coffee from the rather large mug. For the last forty-five minutes we would enjoy the breeze and beautiful views of this magnificent countryside. My thoughts right now were solely focused on Keri. She was every bit as beautiful as I remember. I thought about the photo Angelina sent. Would Keri find me attractive? My hair that was once dark in my younger years now had some streaks of silver mixed in, my face slightly weathered from a life of being in the sun and age itself. Would she still be attracted to and interested in the sixty-year-old me?

I was being tough on myself, almost feeling like a teenager about to ask a girl on a date for the very first time.

But Keri was no ordinary woman. Although our experience was short lived, she is the only woman out of all those I've dated that has never left my thoughts. The instant connection we had was like no other I have ever experienced, and now, after all these years, I am going to hear her voice again.

I glanced over at Angelina, who was focused on watching the sailboats in a distance. I smiled without her noticing, so extremely impressed by the effort she put into making this happen. If left up to me, Keri may have just remained a momentous experience tucked away and concealed deep within the memory bank of my mind, along with too many unanswered, what ifs.

I stood up to see if the docks were coming into view and they were. I picked up the check the waitress had left under the napkin holder and peeled off enough cash to cover it as well as a generous tip and handed it to her as she passed by.

Angelina effortlessly slipped her backpack through her arm allowing it to rest comfortably on her back. I picked up my carry case and we slowly walked towards the other end of the boat where we would exit shortly as the boat docked.

Several members of the cruise line staff were waiting on the dock to secure the boat. I could hear the motor kick down to a slight humming giving us just enough power to drift in.

As we exited, I handed the young baggage handler my ticket. He ducked into the small holding room and within seconds emerged with our suitcases. I thanked him and handed him a tip.

The wonderful aroma of foods being cooked in the various cafes consumed us as we walked along the dock heading towards the car.

"Smells so good." Angelina commented as she closed her eyes and exaggerated inhaling through her nose.

"It sure does. Maybe we should get something for dinner."

"Sure."

"How about we get some meat that's already cooked and sauce, then I can just make pasta?"

"Perfect. And bread too."

"Of course, bread."

We passed several cafés and stores until reaching one of my favorites.

Nobody was in line, so we approached the counter.

"Buongiorno signora."

"Buongiorno." She replied back

"Can I have six meatballs, six sweet sausages, and six bracciole."

"Si."

"What are bracciole?" Angelina asked with a confused expression.

"They are thin steak rolls, seasoned with parmesan cheese, olive oil, salt and pepper, and a few other ingredients. I think you will like them. Why don't you go get a loaf of bread while were waiting?"

"OK."

By the time Angelina came back the woman had everything wrapped up. I got a quart of marinara sauce and we checked out.

My car was parked right around the corner in a lot operated by the marina. We loaded it up with our luggage and groceries then stopped to pay the attendant.

As we made our way home Keri was scrolling on her phone.

"Any response from Keri yet?"

"I was just checking. Not yet, it was my friend."

It was another beautiful sunny day, so my grandfather retracted the roof allowing the warm wind to blow my hair around. I love that.

I have missed Lucia these last few days and my visit will be coming to an end before I know it.

"I think I'm going to hang out with Lucia until dinner okay?"

"Sure. That will also give me some time to catch up on emails and business."

I also wanted to work on that information I promised David. I have been going over my plan of action to help him ever since meeting him for dinner.

When I take Angelina back home in a few weeks I will plan to meet him in DC since I already have a few appointments scheduled there.

The vineyard was now coming into view and from a distance I could see a large delivery truck leaving the gates and heading in the opposite direction towards the next town.

I am assuming the oak barrels had arrived, and ahead of schedule. When the Martones and I decided on the expansion and increased production I got a jump on ordering the barrels. Oak is ideal and the most expensive but also hard to acquire on such short notice.

Franco's wine making knowledge made it quite clear, oak is the way to go, especially for red wines. Wine benefits from storage in oak barrels in two ways. Barrel aging offers controlled oxidation, and inside the oak are several complex chemicals that add to the flavor and texture of the wine. Everything is a science, down to the barrel its stored in. The type of oak and the age of the tree. That is why Franco was at my side when ordering them and I am sure he fully inspected them before accepting the delivery.

As I keyed in the code, I could see Angelina perk up. She was looking forward to seeing her friend and socializing with someone her own age.

She was scanning the grounds as we drove up the driveway.

As we got closer to the Martone's home we could see Lucia and her older sister Antonella sitting on their front porch.

"Can you drop me off grandpa?"

"Of course."

I waved to the three girls as I pulled away and slowly drove up to my house. This time alone would be well spent making a few calls and gathering information that could be helpful to David.

I have several reliable and trustworthy friends working for the Canadian Security Intelligence Service (CSIS) that would be more than willing to assist me.

Before making any calls or internet connections I make certain my customized high-speed VPN is connected, ensuring secure encryption between my device and the end site.

This is one way intelligence officers communicate with each other besides using encrypted dialect and codes.

After making several calls I had valuable information to pass along to David.

Feeling relieved, I now skimmed though a few hundred emails, most meaningless sales ads that slip through filters.

I could feel my anxiety levels rising concerning Keri. Wondering if she had responded to Angelina. Anticipating a phone call with her. Wondering if those same fiery feelings would overtake us as they did so many years ago. Would her beautiful southern accent still have that same spell over me and halt the breath passing in and out of my lungs as it did while standing at that elevator when I was 23.

I remember her just as she was at 18 and have no idea what the mature version of her is now. She had strong Christian values and came from a Christian family. She was so loving, innocent, kind, and her personality had a positive effect on everyone around her.

Would she ever be able to accept me for the things I have done in my life? My career had transformed me into a different person. In the realm of faith and religion I have broken all or certainly most of the ten commandments. My wife divorced me for some of these reasons, and I have never had another solid relationship. I have acquired the ability through extensive training and real-life experiences to pretend to be just about anyone I choose to become but that is not how I want to approach things with Keri. It can be so difficult to turn off the spy mindset and just be yourself. At times, remembering my old self and who I really was is difficult.

Most of my colleagues that were married have been divorced, some several times, many have never married and just have sporadic relationships that never seem to go anywhere, and others have several relationships going on throughout the country or countries.

Just then I hear a door slam.

"Grandpa... Grandpa!"

I jump up and swing open the office door to see if Angelina was Okay.

"Yes, what's wrong?"

She stopped and paused to catch her breath.

"She responded, she messaged me."

I smiled a sign of relief that nothing serious had happened. The way she burst into the house and yelling I was not sure if something had happened to her or one of the Martone girls.

By her big smile and enthusiasm, I assumed the response from Keri was a positive one.

"And?"

"And she said you are still the most handsome man she's ever met and would love to talk to you."

A sign of relief came over me as I picked Angelina effortlessly off the ground and gave her a hug.

I lowered her back down.

"You made this happen. I procrastinated for years and you made it happen,"

"You're welcome." She responded in an extremely cute, dignified manner.

She walked over to my desk and peeled a sheet of paper from the small note pad and picked up a pen lying next to it, glancing at her phone she jotted down Keri's phone number, then handed it to me.

"There you go. She said the best time to call is any time after 6pm."

As I looked at the number, I briefly felt like a teenager again about to call a girl for the first time.

"What time is dinner?"

"Are you hungry?"

"Starving."

"OK let me wrap things up in here and I'll start dinner."

"Sounds great. I'm going to take a quick shower. We were running around playing frisbee."

"OK."

I sat back in my chair and looked out the window. I was now feeling very optimistic and looking forward to calling Keri.

Perhaps I should wait until tomorrow since its already 9:30pm in Florida and I am about to make dinner. I do not want to rush our first conversation.

As I was boiling the water for pasta and simmering the meats and sauce, Angelina walked out. She had her PJs on already and her long hair was wet and in a ponytail.

138

"Would you mind messaging Keri and letting her know I will call her tomorrow."

"Sure!"

So, as my grandfather prepared dinner I went and sat on the sofa and messaged Keri.

Angelina:

"Hi! My grandfather is so happy you liked the picture and would like to talk to him.

It got a little late with us traveling back home and 6-hour time difference so he would like to call you tomorrow evening if that's OK with you?"

I left the chat open as I started a new one with my mom letting her know once again what a great time I had at the resort and just how cool my grandfather really is. I also decided to tell her about connecting with a woman from grandpa's past and promised I would tell her the entire story when I got back home.

She was a bit taken back about the scheming I was doing behind his back, but I made it clear to her that grandpa is not mad, and he is happy I did what I did.

Just then I got a new message alert from Keri, so I immediately switched over to that chat.

Keri:

"Hi! That is fine. Tell him it's no rush. The six-hour difference is significant. It is almost 10pm here and just 4pm there.

I am incredibly happy to hear he is looking forward to speaking with me. For all these years I assumed he just forgot about me. Tell him tomorrow night is perfect, I'm looking forward to it."

Angelina:

"No way, he never forgot about you! Yes, it is almost 4pm here and we are just about to have dinner. I will tell him what you said! Bye!"

Keri:

"Good night!"

"Grandpa, Keri said she totally understands and looks forward to your call tomorrow night."

"Thank you, my little assistant, now come on over here and let's eat."

I said goodnight to my mother as well and closed out our chat. I miss my parents very much, but I love Italy and spending time with my grandfather.

As we talked and ate dinner, I could see a new side of my grandfather slowly surfacing. I have basically only known one side of him. My dad would always say my grandfather is hardened and a hardcore guy. Being a young girl, I did not really understand what that meant. I know my grandfathers' job is much more important and dangerous than the stories he tells me, and I am sure that's what my father was talking about, without telling me too much. But tonight, I see a softness in his eyes that I have never seen. Throughout my short life he has always done things for me, for my mom and dad, for my aunt Emery, uncle Mark, and my cousin Giovanna, but this weekend, I feel I have finally done something for him.

I let him know how much I enjoyed the bracciole as we cleaned up the kitchen and loaded the dishwasher.

We decided to watch a movie and enjoy a few cookies that have been in the kitchen for over a week now but still fresh.

There were not many movies to choose from. Cable television in Italy is not as extensive as in the states and my grandfather refuses to pay extra for premium online channels because he hardly watches television when he is alone except for maybe the same few channels. So, we sort of agreed on an action-adventure movie that did not really interest me, but I was feeling a little tired and counted on falling asleep early this evening. So, I sprawled out on the sofa and nestled my head onto my grandfather's chest using him as a pillow as I often do, and soon drifted off to sleep.

Chapter 28

When I woke up the next day I was in my bed under the covers. Besides carrying me into bed my grandfather placed my phone on the nightstand just out of arms reach so I would have to get up to get it.

I responded to several of my friends who messaged me as I slept. They miss me and I miss them. I look forward to seeing them soon and hanging out. But I am also enjoying my time here, with my Italian friends.

I quickly changed and walked out of my bedroom. I had plans to eat breakfast then spend the day with Lucia. My grandfather was sitting at the kitchen table sifting through some papers with one hand while holding a cup of coffee with the other.

"Good morning."

"Good morning sleepy head, glad to see you decided to wake up."

"It's only 9:30am."

My grandfather always seems to wake up before me no matter how late he goes to bed.

I fixed a bowl of cereal for myself and poured some apple juice.

"Lucia and I are going to ride the bikes then swim okay?"

"Sure, sounds fun. I have a lot to catch up on around here."

"And your phone call later." I said smiling at him.

"I know, and I cannot wait." He glared back.

I finished up breakfast and put on my running shoes.

"Well, I'm heading down to get Lucia."

"OK you girls have fun and be safe."

"Of course." I smiled back at him.

After Angelina left, I decided to take the UTV down to the storage facility. Where all the wine is kept.

I was hoping Franco was there so we could discuss the new shipment of barrels that arrived yesterday and get any updates since I was gone for a few days.

As luck would have it, I saw his UTV parked outside. We keep this building secured at all times; it's never left unlocked.

I keyed in the code and heard the door unlock. Upon entering I could see Franco in the distance moving the barrels into place with the forklift. As I began walking towards him, he noticed me and turned off the machine.

We greeted each other with a handshake.

"I see the shipment came in, and ahead of schedule."

"Yes. I was just situating them. Excellent quality. This company is known for having the best barrels in the country."

"I'm looking forward to the expansion. I have full confidence in your boys."

Franco just looked at me and smiled. In Italy, to compliment someone's children is quite an honor to the parents.

"Grazie. Me too."

Franco is a man of few words. He says what needs to be said and not much more. His passion is his work and family. I completely respect this.

I left and took a quiet ride through the vineyard to look things over and to clear my mind.

Along the way I saw Salvatore and Angelo each working in separate sections. A wave and a smile from each were enough to tell me everything was okay, and they had no concerns.

As I rounded the end of the vineyard, I could see Angelina and Lucia pedaling away down the path. They stopped and both waved in unison. I waved back and continued to the house.

I resumed my work on the computer as I enjoyed a glass of wine. I felt this would help ease this anxious feeling I was beginning to have as the time neared for me to call Keri.

Chapter 29

It was now 1:45, which meant it was 7:45pm in Florida. I wanted to give her time to get home from work and settle down.

I had Angelina email me a screenshot of her social media profile pic, the same one that she showed me on the boat, so I could look at her face anytime I wanted to.

I went into my photos and opened the picture. Staring at her beautiful face immediately made me reach for the phone and dial her number.

Between the security on my end, the time difference, and being in different countries, the connection took upwards of 20 seconds or more. I quickly took another sip of wine then followed it with a sip of water. I was well prepared to keep my mouth and throat quenched in case we talked for a while.

The line connected finally, and she picked up on the third ring. The moment I heard her say hello, I could feel my heart stop beating. Time seemed to stand still. Her soft voice. Her incredibly beautiful southern accent. It hit me like that very first time 37 years ago on that ship.

"Keri?"

"Oh my God, Anthony!"

"Yes, its me."

"How are you?"

"I'm doing great, how are you?"

"The same. I cannot believe we are talking. Your little granddaughter is such a sweet girl."

"She sure is. And she did all this behind my back, I had no idea."

"I know." She replied, laughing.

Keri's laughter and voice filled me with emotions I haven't felt in many years.

"It is so good to hear your voice Keri, and to know you are healthy and doing well."

"Thank you so much. And it is so good to hear your voice. You have never left my heart Anthony. Not one day has passed that you have not been on my mind, not one."

Hearing her say that stopped my breathing.

"And I have never stopped thinking of you. I don't know whatever happened. I regret us falling out of touch. I tried on my end. I sent letters to your parents' home. I left messages with your college roommate."

"You did?"

"Yes! And when you never wrote back or called me, I just assumed you found a new guy and moved on. I was devastated to be honest because we had such an amazing connection."

"Anthony."

"Yes?"

"Your phone number was disconnected, and you never responded to letters I sent to your apartment."

"But I did. I sent so many letters to your parents' home, letting you know I moved to Virginia. I had my new address as the return on the letters and written in the letter itself as well, along with my new phone number, just to make sure that information would not slip by you. And I left many messages with your college roommate and she would tell me she was writing my new number on the whiteboard you both kept messages on for one another next to your dorm room phone."

"I never got messages on that whiteboard from you, and my parents never passed along any letters from you, and I was going home every Friday and then leaving again Sunday evening for school."

"I don't even know how to react to this. I am not lying to you; I have no reason to. I wanted us to work more than anything."

"I am not saying you are lying. I am wondering if my parents kept the letters from me. They genuinely liked you when they met you on the cruise, but they did not want me to be with a guy from another state. They wanted me to be with a local guy so I would always be close to them. And my roommate was jealous of me for some reason and didn't like me much."

"Would your parents do that? Not give you my letters?"

There was a brief pause. I could hear Keri holding back tears. I heard her clear her throat.

144

"I believe my mom would."

One of my biggest dilemma's is dealing with certain emotions, and now within minutes I am being confronted. I had to be careful. Luckily, my training has prepared me for just about anything, so I immediately switched gears.

"Really? But why?"

"My mom and I are close. She knew my feelings for you because I made them clear to her, and that I would leave to be with you in an instant. That scared her."

At this point she was crying a bit.

"So, your mother and roommate possibly sabotaged our relationship?"

"Yes, but unrelated and obviously for much different reasons."

"Keri I'm sorry. I do not want you to be upset. Let's change the topic. So, how's Florida?"

Through her tears she began laughing.

"I hear they have the best oranges there."

Her laughter increased, as my lame attempt at humor seemed to have lighten the mood.

"I see you still have your sense of humor!"

"I hung onto it somehow." I responded laughing.

"For all these years I wondered why you just allowed things to abruptly end between us. Our connection was like nothing I have ever experienced. And now I find out my mom and college roommate were possibly behind it. And I only shared a room with her for one semester, and we basically never spoke again."

"Are your parents still alive?"

"Yes. They still live in Oklahoma. I talk to them at least once a week to catch up. I am calling my mom when we hang up to confront her and find out the truth,

"It will ease our minds, so we at least know. But, even if she played a part, she was just being a mom who did not want to lose her young daughter. Having a daughter, myself, I totally understand."

"So, what happened after the cruise Anthony, you changed your phone number? Did you move?"

"Yes. I had a job offer with the federal government and had to move to Virginia for training."

"Angelina mentioned you retired from the government, so you stayed there your entire career?"

"Yes."

"Which department or agency did you work for?"

"I started out in sort of a support team of corporate business."

"So, you had to move to Virginia, go through training, and then live there for your job?"

"Yes."

"I remember you had a college degree in accounting, right?"

"Yes."

"Why couldn't you just keep your cell phone?"

"Well, they gave me a new cellphone, so I figured why keep mine and pay for it. That's why I kept telling your roommate to write down my new number and I sent my new address and number in several letters to your parents' home."

"And I never got anything. No letters, except for the very first few, and never a new number from my college roommate"

"So, tell me about you Keri. What happened after college?"

"I made it through two years and then ended up marrying a guy I dated in high school."

"I hope it wasn't that same jerk you mentioned you broke up with before the cruise?"

She immediately began laughing.

"Didn't we nickname him puffs, after the tissues, because you told me how he called you every day in hysterics asking you to take him back?"

"Oh my God you remember that?"

"Yes."

"Yes, I ended up marrying him. I was young and my parents wanted me to marry a local guy. I assumed I would never hear from you again. We had two children, a son and daughter, who eventually got married and gave me three grandchildren. Yes, I'm a grandmother."

"I still cannot think of you as a grandmother. You look so youthful and just as gorgeous as the day I met you."

"Well thank you! And it's hard for me to think of you as a grandfather."

"I heard your husband passed away?"

"Yes, he was hit by a car while riding his bike. A hit and run."

"So, they never found the driver?"

"Never."

146

"Must have been hard on you and your children."

"It was."

"Do you mind me asking what career you pursued or what line of work you are involved with?"

"Not at all. Well, I was a stay-at-home mom for many years. Then as the kids got older, I worked several jobs, and eventually I opened a small tanning salon here in Florida."

"That is awesome. The woman with the most amazing tan skin ever running a tanning salon, no marketing needed." I responded laughing.

My laughter was joined by hers.

"Then after doing much research on spray tanning, I incorporated that into my business, which caught on and took off."

"That's awesome, and I'm sure it's much healthier for the skin than tanning booths."

"It so is. But people still have their preferences, so I kept a few booths and transformed a few rooms for spray tanning."

"And do you spray tan clients as well?"

"Yes, I have had all the training, but these days I have several girls working for me that handle the sprays. My passion became focused on creating my own line of sunless solutions."

"Wow amazing!"

"Yes, it's been a long grueling road. But, two years ago, I launched my own product line and so far, it has done very well, business continues to grow and that's a good thing!"

"So, you now actually make the tanning solutions that spray tan artists use?"

"Yes, my own product line."

"Keri, do you realize you actually began making your own tanning solutions when you were still a teenager? I remember on the cruise you had this little secret unmarked plastic bottle with solution in it."

"OH MY GOD YOU REMEMBER THAT?" Her voice rising then going into a fit of laughter.

"Yes, and if my memory serves me correctly it was iodine mixed with baby oil."

"YES."

Her laughter was contagious and instantly made me laugh as well.

"Well, it certainly worked on you and your friend Tonia, you both had the most amazing tans on that ship."

"I'm sure between running the salon and solution business you are kept pretty busy?"

"Oh, for sure, but I've learned how to manage, and I have several excellent dedicated employees that make it all run smooth."

"Good employees are so crucial to any business."

"Oh, for sure." She remarked.

"Enough about me, let's talk about this vineyard of yours in Italy."

I hate talking about myself, but considering I am speaking with Keri, it is a huge exception.

"Well, I retired from the government and had planned a month-long trip to Italy. Not to visit the famous tourists' attractions, I have done that before. But to visit the smaller towns and countryside villages. I rented a villa and car and each day drove into a nearby town to see how the people of Italy truly lived. My father's parents both came from Italy so for me this was significant. One night I ran into an older gentleman at a local restaurant and since we were the only two at the bar we began talking."

"Do you speak Italian?"

"Living here, I've gotten much better. The smaller towns and villages have their own dialect which are much different from the actual Italian language."

"Oh Ok."

"His English was very broken, but the bartender helped interpret the words we got hung up on. He was selling the vineyard that was in his family for three generations. We worked out a deal and within a few weeks the vineyard was mine."

"Wow Anthony that is an amazing story!"

"I knew nothing about running a vineyard, but sort of adopted a family that came with the deal, who know every aspect of running it."

"So, it worked out well?"

"Yes. So far, it has been an amazing experience. Much different than my government job or life in the states."

"So, you just packed up and moved to Italy, just like that?"

"Yes, just like that."

"But what about your children and grandchildren, you're so far away."

"That is a problem. But I travel to the states a few times a year to visit them. These last two years I have gone to get Angelina and bring her back here with me for a month, which has been so nice. I adore that little girl."

"She seems so adorable and truly loves and cares for you Anthony."

"Thank you."

"And your wife? Or ex-wife."

"I've been divorced for about nineteen years now."

"That's quite a long time Anthony. And never remarried?"

"No."

"I'm sure you have some beautiful Italian lady that you date?"

"No." I said, with a slight laugh.

"I find that hard to believe."

"It's true."

"So, you have two children as well?"

"Yes. My son Vincent is Angelina's dad, he is married to Marla and they live in Connecticut. And my daughter Emery is married to Mark and they live in Colorado and have a daughter Giovanna, my other granddaughter."

"Are both granddaughters too much to handle?" She asked in a cute but sarcastic manner.

"No." I replied laughing. "Giovanna is just eight. I will give it a few years then convince my daughter to let me bring her here for a summer."

"Where in Florida do you live?"

"St. Petersburg."

"Is that near Tampa Bay?"

"Yes, very close."

"A good friend of mine lives in Tampa Bay. I visited him years ago."

"How many years ago?"

"Maybe 9-10."

"I was here then. We moved here from Oklahoma about 20 years ago for my husband's job."

"Would have been amazing if our paths crossed then."

149

"I drive to Miami a few times each year, simply to enjoy the ocean, and shop at the amazing stores, it's so beautiful there. Each time, I go to that very same harbor, where the cruise ships come into, where our cruise ship docked 37 years ago. It was the last time I ever saw you."

Her voice became soft and suddenly very emotional.

"I would just look out on the bay and wonder if you were on one of those ships. If you were coming back to me after all these years. I would sit and just sob, wondering what we could have had. I'd leave with my head pounding from crying so hard."

I found her words, so full of deep emotion and innocence, resounding through my usual hardened emotional state.

"I've missed you Keri. Not one day has passed that you haven't entered my thoughts."

"I've missed you to. No matter what life has thrown at me, good times and bad, you have always lived in my greatest memories."

"I want to see you Keri."

"I want to see you to."

"I am bringing Angelina home in 2 weeks. Flying into Connecticut then flying to Washington DC for a few days."

"Can I visit you in Florida?"

There was a slight pause and I wondered if I sounded too pushy.

"Hang on, just checking my calendar. I have a full seven-day sunless convention during that time, in Las Vegas. The events are pretty much 8 hours each day, my evenings would be free, but my daughter and two of my employees are traveling with me."

"I wouldn't want to infringe on your time with them or a work-related conference. You will be busy."

"I totally understand, nor would I want to see you for the first time under such constraints. But I would love to visit Italy again."

Suddenly my spirit escalated.

"You would? You would visit me here?"

"Yes, if you invite me."

"Your invited."

"Ha-ha you didn't hesitate for a second Anthony."

"Of course not." I said, with a beaming smile she could not see.

"You visited Italy before?"

"Many years ago, the touristy attractions like in Rome and Venice."

"Did you like it?"

"Loved it. Loved the culture, and of course the food and wine."

"Keri, when could you come here?"

"How about after my convention?"

"Perfect."

We exchanged email addresses and cell phone numbers as we planned an exact date for her to visit.

"Would you be able to stay for at least a week or more? I know you have a busines to run."

"Yes, I think a week would be great. Are you sure about this?"

"I could not be more sure."

"Wonderful."

"I just sent you a text with the airport to fly into, and once you reserve the flight just let me know which number and arrival time so I can be waiting there for you."

"I will."

"Keri, why don't you let me cover the cost of the flight."

"Thank you, Anthony. That is so thoughtful but not necessary, besides, I can write it off as a business expense."

We both laughed in unison.

"Just got your text, thank you!"

"You are welcome!"

"Just to be clear, my town is very low key, small, quiet, not much going on."

"Anthony…Anthony…."

She interrupted.

"Yes?"

"I don't care about that. I wouldn't care if we were the only two people in the entire town with just a few vending machines for meals and drinks."

I was smiling so big on the other end of that phone as I listened to her continue.

"I have missed you for 37 years, hoping and praying that one day our paths will somehow, someway cross again. I just want to see you and look into your eyes and feel what I did when I was 18. That calmness, that security and protectiveness that I felt in your presence and in your arms. That comfortableness we shared as we talked into the wee hours of the morning. I don't need busy streets or endless stores and restaurants; I just need to be with you."

This conversation has spun emotions inside me that I no longer thought even existed.

"Keri. That was beautiful."

"Well, it's just how I feel."

"I feel you and I can talk forever and never run out of things to say."

"I feel the same exact way." I responded back.

"But we should probably call it a night. I know you have your granddaughter."

"She keeps me busy for sure."

"So, I will go online and search for flights tomorrow and email you with the information okay."

"Perfect. I cannot wait to see you Keri."

"I can't wait to see you Anthony."

"Good night."

I hesitated for a second, not wanting the conversation to end. I could listen to her soft beautiful southern voice forever. Finally, giving in, I had to acknowledge the conversation was ending.

"Good night Keri."

Chapter 30

As I laid the phone back onto the base, I felt a numbing sensation, as if I were in a dreamlike state.

I was still trying to comprehend that fact that I would be seeing Keri in just a few short weeks.

That tranquil state of mind was about to be disrupted by my granddaughter as I could hear her trying to tiptoe up to my office door.

"Come on in Angelina, we just hung up."

She swung open the office door and had the biggest smile on her face as she walked over to me and hopped up to sit on the corner of my massive oak desk.

"Soooooo?"

Her eyes opened wide, and she had the most adorable expression.

"It went amazing!" I said, as she shot her arm up into the air as if she just won first place at a sporting event.

"I have good news and bad news, which would you like first."

"The good news."

"Keri is coming here, to visit me."

Angelina's expressions were priceless, as she appeared just as excited as I was.

"And the bad news?"

"It's hard for me to tell you this, but she's coming after I bring you back home."

She exaggerated a sad face which made me crack up laughing, then quickly converted it back to a happy face.

"That's okay grandpa, my job is completed."

Once again, she had me laughing so hard.

"If all goes well, I will meet her someday."

"That's true."

"Grandpa you should take her to the resort you and I just went to."

"Do you know I was thinking that very thought. She is coming for a week so spending a few days there would be wonderful, especially since there isn't much going on around this town."

Angelina smiled.

"She's going to email me her flight information asap and then I can make plans on this end."

"She will love that resort."

"She so will."

"Well, I am ready for dinner. Let's have something simple and easy then watch a movie, sound good?"

"Sounds good."

"Breakfast food? Cereal? Scrambled eggs?"

"Cereal for me."

We sat down and had cereal. After two bowls I was still a little hungry and decided to have two slices of partially stale bread.

After showers we met on the sofa. I scrolled through the channels looking for anything remotely interesting that we both might enjoy, eventually settling for *When Harry met Sally*, a movie I love but may not be so enjoyable for a 12 yr. old.

As Angelina laid across the sofa so peacefully while using me as a pillow, I myself felt a calmness come over me that I have not felt in quite some time. Still trying to process the fact that I will soon be face to face with Keri.

Angelina was not able to stay awake for the entire movie, so after it ended I turned off the TV and carried her to bed.

Tonight, I would pass on a glass of wine and simply retire to bed. Keri was the only thing on my mind, and I was hoping for something I have not experienced or remembered in many years, a wonderful dream.

Chapter 31

Morning always seems to come quickly. Since I did not set an alarm, I was woken up by the brightness of the sun cresting through my semi closed curtains.

Angelina once again had a bowl of cereal as I simply enjoyed a cup of coffee. Her and Lucia had plans to ride bikes and swim, while I would work in the office.

As my email loaded, I was pleasantly surprised to see an email from Keri.

Anthony,

I cannot express how happy I am that we connected and had such a wonderful conversation last night, hearing your voice brought me right back to the past, in a good way. Missing you and wondering whatever happened between us has carried a burden in my heart for all these years. Last night, after we hung up, I called my mother and asked her about your letters and phone calls. She broke down crying and confessed that she discarded every letter you mailed to me after the first few. She told me how she opened and read a few of them and was so scared I would leave town to be with you, and she did not want to lose me. She told me how you professed falling in love with me and how you wanted me to move to Virginia to be with you. By that point I too was crying. I was so incredibly angry at her for taking away a part of my life she had no business taking. Her crying woke my dad, and I could hear him in the background asking if everything was ok. Through her tears and shortness of breath, no doubt to the anxiety brought on by this confrontation, she kept telling me she knew one day you would come for me and she would be faced with this lie she kept hidden all these years. Over and over, she confessed how sorry she was and asked me to forgive her. It was awful. It left both my parents and me terribly upset. Before hanging up the phone I did forgive her. I am so sorry this happened Anthony.

On a more uplifting note, LOL, I was able to make a flight reservation. I hope it is not too stressful on you, but I made it for two days after you return home from the states. Talk soon!

Hugs,
Keri

My response was simple.

Keri,

There was nothing better than waking up to an email from you! I am so sorry you had that blowout with your mom last night. I feel your anger, I truly do.

It was so long ago, we cannot change the past, but we can create our own future, with no interference. It was best to forgive her, she sounds very remorseful.

Your arrival date is perfect. I cannot believe it's just a few weeks away.

I will be waiting for you at the airport, but of course I hope we can talk or email before then!

Hope you have a great day!
~Anthony

Chapter 32

The next nine days passed by quickly and soon Angelina was hugging Lucia and Antonella goodbye. My home will soon return to its quiet old boring self without the youthful energy of my little angel.

I had already told Franco I would be gone for a few days and to have Isabella reach out to me should anything of concern arise.

As we drove off heading to the airport, I tried to interject some positivity into Angelina's sad demeanor.

"I know it's hard leaving your friends here, but at the same time you are returning to your other friends back home. I know it doesn't make this any easier, but it's something to look forward to."

She turned her head and gave me a smile.

"I mean, how do you think I feel? I'm losing my sidekick and my little intel officer."

That got her to laugh.

"Thanks to me you won't be alone for very long grandpa."

"That's true. Keri flies here in a few days. We have been emailing every day. Right now, she is in Las Vegas at a convention with her daughter."

"For her business?"

"Yes."

The small airport was quiet, and we boarded very quickly. I always try to get direct flights to and from the states because I cannot stand being on a plane more than 10-11 hours.

When we arrived in Connecticut my son and Marla were waiting in baggage claim. As soon as Angelina spotted them, she took off running and jumped into my son's arms for a big hug as Marla rubbed her back.

As I approached, they greeted me, and Marla gave me a hug. My son and I exchanged a custom handshake.

We all walked over to the baggage carousel and waited until we spotted Angelina's two suitcases. I had everything I needed in my carry-on, since I was only staying in DC for two nights.

They both had so many questions for Angelina. Even though the long flight was draining coupled with her missing Italy and her friends there, she still managed to enthusiastically answer every question.

Her and I were still on Italy time, but here in Connecticut it was after 1am.

Still to this day, the relationship between my son and I seems more like business than a father/son relationship, and I know that is all on me.

"So, dad, your flight leaves in 2 hours?"

"Yes."

"I'm sorry it's so early in the morning, there's nothing we can really do. I wish you could have come and stayed with us at least for the night."

"Me too. But this was the only flight I could get to DC."

"I understand dad."

"Well don't let me hold you up. Go home and get some sleep. I hope to see you all for Christmas."

I gave Angelina one more hug, lifting her off the ground I whispering to her.

"Thank you so much for spending this past month with me. And thank you for becoming a pretty savvy intel officer and connecting me with Keri."

We all laughed.

"That's a pretty amazing story dad. You met this woman on a cruise when you were just 23?"

"Yes."

"Marla did a little spying of her own after Angelina told her the good news and gave her this woman's name."

"Really?"

"I wasn't spying Vincent, I just visited her social media page, simply to see what she looked like. And woah, she is gorgeous."

"I told you she was mom."

"I'm happy for you dad. You deserve to be happy. It's been a long time."

By long time, he was referring to the years I have been divorced from his mother.

"Thank you, son."

"And she's coming to visit you? You already made plans?" Marla asked.

"Yes. She's actually flying to Italy in a few days, right after I return."

"Enjoy that time with her!"

"Thank you, Marla."

"Grandpa."

"Yes angel?"

"It's okay if she uses my bedroom."

"Are you sure you don't mind? I have other rooms."

"No, it's fine, plus the bed is really comfortable."

Giving her one last hug.

"Ok angel I will offer it to her."

"Goodbye Marla!" I said, giving her a departing hug.

I then reached out to shake my sons' hand once again.

"Goodbye son!"

I watched them walk away as they made their way towards the exit. All three turned and waved one last time before disappearing through automatic doors leading into the parking area.

I turned and walked away from the baggage claim area stepping onto the nearby escalator which took me up to an area where at least one bar was open for us late night or early morning travelers to sit, relax, and have a drink.

After two glasses of wine, I made my way to board the plane. It would be a quick flight, just about 63 minutes, then a 15-minute cab ride to the hotel and I would be able to sleep until noon since my first meeting is not until 3pm.

At this time in the morning my flight to DC was for the most part empty, I counted six of us total. The one flight attended appeared to be exhausted and barely going through the motions.

I am looking forward to these meeting being over and returning to Italy and patiently await Keri's arrival.

I took Angelina's advice and already arranged a three-day escape to that same resort for Keri and I.

Chapter 33

My business in DC has concluded and I am back at the airport about to board my direct flight back to Italy.

Keri and I continue to send either a text or email every day. I have not had this closeness with a woman in so long, and I am loving it.

I am feeling that same connection I had with her 37 years ago.

After almost 9 hours in the air, we began descending upon Verona airport. This flight back was a little more difficult for me. I miss Angelina. The relationship between my son and I continues to weigh on my mind. Wondering what I can do to break down that wall I built years ago. Wanting us to have a more comfortable father/son relationship and not feel like he is a business associate of mine every time I am around him.

I exit the plane and walk briskly to my car. Since Keri is arriving in just two days I decided to stop in town and stock up on food, snacks, and drinks.

I never thought to ask her what she likes to eat because we always seem to find other more interesting topics to discuss. Three of the nights we will be at the resort, then I figure a few nights we can eat in town or an adjacent town, and maybe a few nights I will cook for her. Hope she likes steak, chicken, or pasta, since my culinary skills do not extend much further.

As I arrived home, Franco and Maria were relaxing on their front porch, no doubt after having a delicious meal prepared by Maria. I pulled up as Franco walked down off the porch to greet me.

"How was your trip to the United States?"

"It was nice Franco, but I already miss my little Angelina."

"Si, my girls miss her as well."

"How is everything around here?"

"Benissimo." *(very well)*

"Excellent."

"I have a friend coming to visit me from the states, a woman. She will be with me for a week, but we will be out of town for a few of those days."

Franco's English is not that great, and I can see him searching to put my words together and make sense to him.

"Oh, a signorina."

"Si," I responded

After saying good night to both I drove off and went to my home. I carried in the two bags of groceries and packed the perishables away in the refrigerator. After a month of Angelina being here, the home has now returned to its deafening quiet state.

These two days passed quickly, and I found myself trying to sleep the night before Keri was arriving. I stared at the ceiling as so many thoughts and memories swirled around in my head.

Chapter 34

I was startled out of a deep sleep to the blaring of my alarm clock. Thankfully, I fell asleep, but I am not even sure what time I did.

I have anticipated this day for the last few weeks. Keri's plane is due to arrive in just a few hours.

Before shaving and showering, I go through the entire house just to make sure everything is neat and clean, which is how I always keep it, but this was to put my mind at rest.

I walked out onto the deck and turned on the robotic pool vacuum so it would be spotless for when I returned with Keri. The jacuzzi is always covered when not being used so I was not concerned with that.

I already did a few loads of laundry, making sure to put fresh sheets and blanket on the bed in Angelina's room, as well as towels in that bathroom, which was equipped with a shower and sunken tub for baths, which Angelina loved to take and would sometimes be in that tub for an hour.

Now that the house was in order it was time to shower and get dressed. The high temperature for today was going to be 82 degrees so I decided to dress as I usually do, casual attire. A nice pair of jeans and short sleeve button up navy-blue shirt.

I took a bottle of water for the drive and connected my phone to the Bluetooth so I could listen to songs from my playlist to sooth the slight anxious feeling I was experiencing. I slowly backed my car out of the garage, the top was still down from the day before.

I stopped at the end of the driveway, and once again read the text Keri sent me this morning before she flew out, as the gates opened.

I scrolled through my playlist until I reached a song that has reminded me of Keri ever since I first heard it. It is such an amazing and powerful song by the incredibly talented singer Adele.

I hit play and cranked up the volume, then dropped it into first gear and slowly pulled away from the gates. The music started as I watched the gates closing behind me, now dropping it into second gear.

Everybody loves the things you do
From the way you talk
To the way you move
Everybody here is watching you
'Cause you feel like home
You're like a dream come true
But if by chance you're here alone
Can I have a moment?
Before I go?
'Cause I've been by myself all night long
Hoping you're someone I used to know
You look like a movie
You sound like a song
My God this reminds me, of when we were young

Shifting into 4th gear, cruising down the countryside roads this song is taking me back to that moment on the cruise when I first saw Keri. The way she captured me from the very first time our eyes met.

Let me photograph you in this light
In case it is the last time
That we might be exactly like we were
Before we realized
We were scared of getting old
It made us restless
It was just like a movie
It was just like a song
I was so scared to face my fears
Nobody told me that you'd be here
And I'd swear you moved overseas
That's what you said, when you left me

Images of us on that ship keep flashing before my eyes. The younger versions of us. The way she looked at me, smiled at me, and how it felt to pull her close and kiss her.

163

You still look like a movie
You still sound like a song
My God, this reminds me, of when we were young

As I am getting closer to the airport, I see a Delta flight off in the distance and know she has to be on it. I feel the blood now pumping through my body as Adele's powerful voice vibrates through every vein.

Let me photograph you in this light
In case it is the last time
That we might be exactly like we were
Before we realized
We were sad of getting old
It made us restless
It was just like a movie
It was just like a song
When we were young
(When we were young)
When we were young
(When we were young)
It's hard to win me back
Everything just takes me back
To when you were there
To when you were there
And a part of me keeps holding on
Just in case it hasn't gone
I guess I still care
Do you still care?

The plane has landed already as I pull into the airport, the song still blaring as I am dropping gears to slow down. Between the powerful sound of the custom dual exhausts while down shifting and Adele's voice, the few people outside just stop and stare.

It was just like a movie
It was just like a song
My God, this reminds me
Of when we were young

When we were young
(When we were young)
When we were young
(When we were young)
Let me photograph you in this light
In case it is the last time
That we might be exactly like we were
Before we realized
We were sad of getting old
It made us restless
Oh I'm so mad I'm getting old
It makes me reckless
It was just like a movie
It was just like a song
When we were young

Not taking any chances that she may be waiting without me there; I pull up to the valet just as the song ends. I put it in neutral, pull the brake, and kill the engine. One of the valets is beginning to walk towards me as I toss him the key and tell him to keep it close because I will not be long.

I briskly walk into the airport and glance down towards the baggage claim area. The carousel is already moving which tells me the passengers are leaving the plane. I get on the escalator that leads up to the gates and as I am about to reach the top, my head just cresting to where I can see people moving about, I see Keri, and my eyes become focused solely on her. My legs instinctively step off the escalator because my brain was not communicating with my body at that moment. I slowly took a few steps while my eyes remained glued to her. She noticed me at the exact same moment, and she stopped as well. Flashbacks to the very first time seeing her on that ship echoed through my mind, the Adele song, soaking her in, millisecond by millisecond, my heart racing the same way it did at 23, for a moment time stood still.

I then began to walk towards her, as her hands released the two carry-on bags, dropping them at her sides, but she did not move. She was even more gorgeous, more breathtaking in person. I was so taken by her, while experiencing an overwhelming adrenaline rush throughout my entire body. I reach her and she falls into my arms at

165

the very moment I extend them, we embrace, and I lift her off the ground and spin her around. This makes her laugh revealing those familiar beautiful white teeth and enticing smile. I gently lower her back to the ground as our eyes meet. With no words even spoken yet, I placed a gentle kiss on her lips. Her hypnotic bluish-green eyes spoke to me the same way they did 37 years ago. I remember every detail of her face as if it were yesterday.

For once in my life, or at least since I became an intelligence officer, I was unaware of my surroundings, and surprisingly, I was not alarmed by it.

We stood right there, fully embraced, hugging and kissing like two people who just instantly fell in love again. Our bodies molded together so naturally. The scent of her perfume captivated me. This instant bond and genuine affection were reassurance enough that we could never be apart again. At that moment, I knew that this journey back into her arms was in fact my destiny. After 37 years, this was undoubtedly a kiss worth waiting for.

~The End